Bella's Hope

A Map for Bella, Book 1

PAULA KAY

DEDICATION

To Cristina.
Thank you for your friendship, love, support
and the many bookstore/coffee/dessert meet-up memories. ☺

TABLE OF CONTENTS

CHAPTER 1

Isabella Dawson looked up from her laptop, aware of her friend's presence as Jemma stared intently at her from the doorway.

"You look great, Jem. Hot date?"

"No. No date. Just going out with the girls we met at the cafe yesterday." Jemma seemed to be eyeing her carefully before she continued. "Come with us, Bella. Seriously, you've been working nonstop and—"

"I can't." Isabella cut her friend off. "You know how close I am to finishing."

Jemma was nodding her head, but it was an argument the two had been having more and more, lately, during their travels.

"I know. I know, but Bella—it's Paris." Jemma gestured toward the window where they had the most stunning view of the Eiffel Tower.

Isabella took in a deep breath. If she was being honest with herself, she knew that she'd become more than a bit obsessed with finishing her book. Despite the changing landscape outside their rented apartments, finishing the book seemed to be all she thought about these days—well, that and the much anticipated upcoming meeting with her birth father, Lucas. The sudden thought made her heart pound faster.

"I know. You're probably right, but I'm just having a hard time relaxing—thinking about the deadline and—and everything."

"Your self-imposed deadline, you mean."

Isabella felt her face go hot. She'd come a long way since high school—since her trip to Italy only months ago—but shaking her perfectionist tendencies was proving harder than she'd anticipated.

"Yeah, I know. What can I say?" She laughed lightly, willing her friend to understand.

True to form, Jemma crossed the room to put her arms around Isabella, giving her a quick kiss on top of her head. "I know. I get it. And you're right. It is important. I know you want to publish it before Christmas. I'm cheering you on—promise."

The two hugged and Isabella thought about how lucky she was—for about the millionth time since she and Jemma had begun their European journey together, months earlier. She and Jemma were so different in many ways—Jemma was definitely the free spirit of the two—but somehow they'd made an unbelievable connection and now Isabella couldn't imagine her life without her new best friend.

"You're a great cheerleader. It means a lot to me. Truly. And I'm actually hoping to be done before London—before we meet Thomas. If I can get the rough draft done in the next week or so, I'll be able to enjoy England and Ireland with you guys. Besides, Thomas would kill me if I spent this much time on my computer when we're finally getting together."

"Well, I can't wait to meet Thomas finally. You guys have talked so much during our trip that I feel like I already know him."

"The video chats have been fun, huh?" No matter how busy things had gotten, Isabella had honored her weekly video chat commitment with both Thomas and her parents back in Connecticut.

"Very fun—especially given how cute that so-called *best friend* of yours is." Jemma winked at her and Isabella laughed in response.

"I'm not sure what I need to do to convince you. Thomas and I are *just* friends. You'll see that when you meet him. He's practically like a brother to me."

"So then you don't care that I find him extremely attractive?"

Jemma was teasing her, but there was no denying the instant feeling the thought caused in Isabella's gut. She didn't know exactly why, but the thought of Thomas liking Jemma in a romantic way caused her stress. Well, they were her two best friends, and potential friction between them wouldn't be good. Isabella hadn't been in many relationships herself, but she knew enough about Thomas's track record to know that his relationships—at least thus far—had known their share of friction.

"Bella." Jemma's nudge brought Isabella out of her thoughts. "You know I'm only joking."

"Well, I'm not sure about Thomas being the right guy for you but I do know that you deserve someone great, Jem."

"As do you." Jemma walked across the room to pick up her handbag from the table. "But neither of us are really looking for relationships on this trip, now are we?" Jemma laughed. "Might I remind you of our pact?"

When they'd started their European adventure a few months earlier, they'd discussed at length their goals for the trip. Besides their mutual desire to explore their creative ideas—Jemma with her painting and Isabella with her writing—they both felt that it was the perfect time in their lives to be selfish, learning more about themselves and what they wanted to do after their big adventure.

And Isabella had the journal from Arianna—the greatest gift that her birth mother had left her when she died. The letters that she'd written to Isabella in that leather-bound book had meant more to Isabella than anything else she held in her possession. She'd not shared those private letters with anyone yet—not even Jemma. Even as she had the quick thought, Isabella knew that the journey she was on was to be shaped not only by the map that Arianna had left her, but by those words her mother had written just for her.

"Hello. Earth to Bella." Jemma's voice interrupted Isabella's thoughts.

"Oh, sorry. Right. The pact." She smiled at her friend as she got up from the desk in the corner of the living room. "We've got plenty of time for boyfriends, right?"

"And plenty of time to just have a little fun. And on that note—don't wait up."

"Jem, be careful, okay?"

"As always." Jemma turned to smile at her as she opened the door. "And if you change your mind, text me."

"Will do. Have fun."

CHAPTER 2

Isabella closed her laptop and crossed the room to
the kitchen to put the teakettle on. She'd gotten into the
ritual of having tea during her nighttime writing sessions
ever since they'd arrived in Paris three weeks earlier. She
sat down at the small table in the breakfast nook to wait
for the water to boil.

When she and Jemma had found the apartment rental
online, they'd both fallen in love with it instantly. The
place had big windows and wonderful little balconies—all
of which revealed the stunning views of the Eiffel Tower
and the beautiful city below. Isabella felt like pinching
herself yet again as she stared out the window.

She'd never in her wildest dreams imagined that she'd
be on this trip of a lifetime to begin with, let alone able to
afford the luxury accommodations that they'd been able
to rent along the way. She hadn't grown up like that. She
was only just starting to understand what it felt like to not
have financial concerns—to have the ability to say yes to
anything, regardless of the price tag.

And she and Jemma had been saying yes to a lot

when it came to their travels. They'd already extended the first part of their trip to include much of France, which was how they'd come to be in Paris. They were both enjoying the inspiration that they'd felt while in Italy and France. Isabella's writing had accelerated and Jemma had painted some of the most beautiful pieces of her life thus far.

They hadn't quite been ready to head to London upon Thomas's arrival there a month earlier, and when Isabella had invited him to join them in Paris, he'd declined. Finally, after much prodding, he'd admitted to the fact that he was quite enamored with a woman he'd met—someone he'd been chatting with online before arriving in London. Isabella couldn't help but roll her eyes as she even thought about the conversation that they'd had about her. He'd even used the word enamored, which had totally thrown her for a loop. She knew that Thomas was probably just having some fun and she'd get the real scoop from him soon enough.

Isabella got up to walk over to the map that they'd tacked up on the wall—Arianna's map—her birth mother's map from so long ago. She used to tear up whenever she'd look at it, but now those tears had been replaced with a fierce determination to make this trip count—to see everything that the young Arianna had never been able to see before she'd died.

Even as she had the thought, it made her feel uncomfortable. Jemma would probably tell a different story. She'd expressed her fears that Isabella was missing out on so much—staying in writing during so many of the days spent in gorgeous European cities. But Jemma hadn't read the letters.

The whistle of the teakettle interrupted Isabella's thoughts. She made her cup of tea and walked back into the living room, placing it on the end table while she went to her bedroom to retrieve the journal. She'd been keeping a journal herself during the trip—just as she'd always done—but tonight she needed to reread the letters from her mother. She needed some fortification for the choices she was making—for the anguish that she was feeling about finishing her book.

She sat back on the comfy sofa and opened the worn leather cover to the pages she'd read more times than she could count since the book had been placed in her hands only a few months earlier. She knew the words by heart, yet she loved to look at her mother's handwriting—she felt connected to her when she read them, something that she knew Arianna had wanted desperately for her daughter.

My Dearest Daughter,

I'm so sorry that these words will never be spoken for you to hear them from my lips. I wanted so badly to meet you one day—to hold you in my arms finally for more than just the short seconds we had together the day that you were born.

I'm sorry that you might have unanswered questions. It was never my intention to not be able to share with you all the thoughts I've ever had about you ever since the day that you were born, but fate had something else in mind, so the words on this page and the words spoken by those closest to me will have to be enough. I pray that it will be.

Where to start...there's so much to say, isn't there?

I want you to know, most of all, that every day I've regretted that I didn't fight harder to keep you. I never wanted to give you up, but I think, given the circumstances, perhaps it has been the best thing for you after all. I've hoped and prayed every day that you've had a good life—that you've felt loved and that you've had everything you could need to be happy.

Your happiness is what drives me daily now as I watch the clock tick toward the end for me.

By the time you are reading this letter, you will have met everyone that has meant so much to me: Gigi—hopefully Douglas is still by her side; her husband if I've had any say in it ;)—Lia (your grandmother), Blu, and Jemma.

My greatest wish now is that you would know them all and be loved by them all in the way that I was—and that they will have the chance to know you too.

I know you might be wondering about your father. I've not spoken a great deal about him to the others. I'm afraid that I've not been fair to him about any of this—your birth or my death. He loved me at one time and he deserved to know about you, but my parents wouldn't allow it while they were alive and—well, I'm sorry to say that I was a coward in that regard. But I think he'd want to know you, so I will leave that to you and in the back of this book, you'll find his name and the last known address and phone number that I have for him. Locating him is something that Douglas can probably help you with if that time should come—and why shouldn't it? You deserve to know the full truth of who you are, my sweet girl.

By now, Douglas will have told you about the trust that I've set up for you and all about the wealth that I'd grown up with. None of it ever really meant that much to me, except I know that it bought me some opportunities in life that I might not have known otherwise. It definitely bought me some special experiences with Lia and with the others—those are the things that have meant the most to me during these last days.

I want you to use the money for your education if that's your wish or your need, but you have my blessing to use it for your dreams—whatever those might be—and truly there is plenty there for everything you could ever want for. I love that I can give that to you now and I only wish that I could be there to share in it all with you.

Do what you like with the things in the box. My intention with each item is that they would help you to have a better sense of who I was and what my dreams were as a young girl. But don't spend one moment worrying about me now. I've come to a total peace about my life and my death. I've forgiven myself even for the decisions made that took you from me. It is only about moving forward now, and this letter to you is a part of all that for me, just as I hope that it will be for you too.

Gigi called me bella ever since I was a small child. I remember asking her why she called me that one time. (And I bet that she is calling you bella now too.) She told me that it meant beautiful and that I was beautiful, but not only on the outside. She said that it was her term for me for all the beauty I possessed inside—some of it yet to be brought out into the world.

So, my dearest daughter, I shall call you Bella—for I know that you are a true beauty, inside and out—preparing to live a life that is full of love and happiness.

That's my wish for you, my sweet Bella.

I love you more than you could ever know.

Your Mother,
Arianna Sinclair

Isabella jumped when she heard her phone ding on the table beside her. She felt shivers up and down her spine when she saw who it was from.

Her father.

She smiled as she opened the text to read it.

CHAPTER 3

Bella, I hope that I'm not disturbing you. Do you have a minute?

Isabella laughed lightly as she punched in a response. *Sure do. What's up?*

Lucas. Her biological father.

She still couldn't believe how fast Douglas had found him. Within two weeks of leaving her grandparents' villa in Tuscany, Douglas had located Lucas and broken the news to him that he had a daughter—that he and Arianna had had a daughter together so many years earlier.

Isabella was surprised at how easy their connection had been. Lucas had, of course, known of Arianna's passing all those years ago—the whole community had known about the young girl's tragic death—but he'd had no idea that she'd given birth to Isabella, no idea that they'd had a beautiful baby girl when he'd been barely a young man himself.

Over the past few months, they'd had numerous voice and video conversations, both of them amazed when they saw one another for the first time—Isabella at how much she looked like her father and Lucas at how much Isabella looked like the young Arianna that he'd loved so long ago. He'd been overcome with emotion the first time he'd seen her on his computer screen, and Isabella loved him instantly for the tears that so easily rolled down his face.

Yes, they'd made quite a connection after many long conversations, and now the only thing left to do was to meet in person, something Isabella knew she was ready for. Her phone dinged again and Isabella glanced down to read the text.

I want to invite you to come to San Francisco—for Thanksgiving if you can make it. Please say you'll come, Bella.

Her heart beat faster when she saw the note. Everything had happened so fast and she had so much going on—with her travels and finishing her book—and she and Jemma were planning to meet everyone in Tuscany for Christmas. Even her parents were going to fly out from Connecticut for the holidays. Could she possibly fit this trip in? It did give her almost three months to finalize everything with her book—and also three months to spend with Thomas.

She paused for a moment, her finger hovering over the button that would send her response across the miles to her father. She thought about Arianna and the letter that she'd just reread again, smiled, and sent the text.

Yes, I'd love to. We'll make it happen.

Great! Annie's going to be so excited. And Kate. We all can't wait to meet you.

Four-year-old Annie. When Isabella had found out that she had a sister, she'd been beside herself with excitement. She'd always wanted one. Watching Jemma and her little sister Kylie together had been the sweetest thing in the world to her. It was hard to believe that in just a few months she'd be meeting them. Kate, Lucas's wife, had been lovely to her every time they'd talked or video chatted. She knew that she'd probably be feeling nervous as the time got closer, but for now she'd just enjoy the anticipation of the meeting.

She pushed her thoughts aside long enough to remember not to keep Lucas waiting for her reply.

I can't wait to meet you all too. Chat next week some time?

Perfect. Night, Bella. Sweet dreams. xo

She smiled as she quickly calculated the time in California and sent off one last text.

Have a good day. xo

Isabella sipped her tea as she thought about her father and everything that had transpired over the past few months. It really was so unbelievable how much her life had changed. She'd gone from being a Harvard-bound high school valedictorian to someone who hadn't given a thought about her academics in weeks—well, other than any agonizing she was doing over her writing. But she felt solid about her decision to defer her enrollment at

Harvard. If she was being completely honest, she really didn't see herself going at all, but time would tell. She'd wait to see how her writing went and if it was something that she felt she wanted to do long-term.

She checked the time, wondering if it was too late to text Thomas. Surely he'd be up—probably out at some fancy London party with his new girlfriend. She bit her lower lip and sent the text off before she could think about it.

Hey, you. Busy?

Her phone dinged in response a few seconds later.

Kinda. What's up?

Darn. She did want to talk to him—to tell him about her plans to meet Lucas, but not if he was with "the girl."

Oh, it can wait. Chat tomorrow? Regular time?

Shoot! Totally spaced and have plans in the afternoon. Can we do it earlier? 9AM?

Isabella grinned. She knew it was rare that Thomas was up that early. If she was being honest with herself, it felt good that he was making the effort, despite forgetting the regularly scheduled chat that they'd been having for the past three months.

Sure. 9 is fine. If you're up for it.

I will be. Miss you tons, Iz.

Isabella smiled at the name she'd not been using for a while now. Only her parents and Thomas still called her by her childhood nickname. The name Bella seemed to come with her new life—given to her by a mother that had never known her and the new terrific extended family that she'd inherited. She liked introducing herself as Bella now, but to Thomas, she was still Izzy. And she liked that as well.

Miss you too, T.

With one more glance at the time, Isabella crossed the room to sit at the desk with the incredible view out the window in front of her. She was tired, but she'd promised herself that she'd complete one more chapter before going to bed.

She took a deep breath and opened her laptop, determined to focus on her characters and the story she was trying to tell—determined to push thoughts about Thomas, Lucas, and everything else aside for the next hour or so.

PAULA KAY

CHAPTER 4

Isabella woke up to the smell of strong coffee and quiet music playing. In general, she liked to get up early herself, so in this regard, she and Jemma did very well sharing an apartment. It was rare that Jemma wasn't up working on a painting before seven o'clock.

Today, like so many days before, Isabella found her friend in the living room—in the second little space next to Isabella's work spot, with equally impressive views and the light streaming in to just perfectly meet Jemma's canvas set up on the easel she traveled with. It was another reason they'd chosen the big apartment—the fact that they both instantly could see themselves working in the shared space.

Jemma looked up from her painting and smiled at Isabella as she walked into the room.

"Morning. Grab a coffee and I'll take a break in a second to join you."

"Morning. Let me see what you're working on first." Isabella grinned back at Jemma and made her way to where her friend was standing in front of the canvas.

"Oh, it's lovely, Jem. One of your best for sure." The painting of the city's skyline in the early morning hours nearly took her breath away. "Will you ship this one to your mom?"

Jemma had been shipping most of her artwork to California when she'd finished, but since they'd been in Paris, Isabella had noticed that she'd been setting a few aside.

"Nope. This one will go to the vineyard—to Lia and Antonio's."

"Ah…Christmas presents." Isabella smiled, thinking about her own gift idea for the upcoming celebration.

Jemma nodded and proceeded to finish up with the color she was working with. "Done. And good timing. Now, let's have a coffee in the kitchen."

The two girls poured themselves coffees and nestled into the little breakfast nook.

"So, tell me about last night. How was it? Did you go out dancing? Meet any cute boys?" Isabella winked at her friend.

"No, no boys. And no dancing either, I'm afraid. I'm saving that for when you *do* want to come out." Jemma laughed.

On the rare occasions that Isabella had gone out late at night during their travels, the two girls had had the best times dancing the night away. Jemma claimed that Isabella was her favorite dance partner and Isabella felt the same. It was the one time she really did let her hair down a bit.

She'd never been one to go to parties or dances during high school, so to discover how much she loved moving to the hip European music had been a great surprise to her.

"I will do it. I promise. I just have a few more chapters to write before it will be a good time to take a break."

"Good. I'm holding you to it." Jemma laughed and Isabella noticed something different about her friend as the light struck her hair through the window.

"Hey, your hair. You found a place?"

Jemma laughed. "Yeah, one of the girls had recommended someone to me and I got in at the last minute yesterday. Do you like it?"

One of the things Isabella greatly admired about Jemma was her willingness to be different, always changing her look, whether she was getting her hair chopped off or trying out a whole different wardrobe. Now Isabella reached over to run her fingers through the wide pink streak in her friend's shoulder-length blonde hair.

"I didn't notice it last night with it up. Yeah, it's great, Jem. I love it. You'll have to let me know where—I could use a trim myself." She reached down to grab a section of her straight brown hair. "I know I've got some split ends that need to be dealt with."

"I think you should try something different. Maybe going blonde would perk you up a little bit."

"As if it were that easy, right?" Isabella laughed at her friend's suggestion. "Maybe one day I'll try something new, but now is not that time, my friend."

The two laughed, sipping their coffees at the same time.

"So how was your night? Did you get a lot of writing done?"

"Yeah. I got another chapter written. Oh, something did happen that was pretty exciting."

"Do tell." Jemma leaned forward in her chair.

"Well, Lucas—my father—texted me, asking if I'd come to San Francisco for Thanksgiving."

"Great! I assume you said yes?"

"I did, although I do have a lot to get done before then. Well, okay, not exactly true. I'll be done with the book and enjoying some travel adventures with my two besties around that time. But yeah, I told him that I'd work it out. I think it's important."

"I'll say. It's so exciting! And you're going to meet that cute little sister of yours."

Isabella had introduced Jemma to everyone during one of their video chat sessions. "Yep. Oh, and you're invited. I mean I'm sure it would be fine with them and I don't want to leave you alone—well, unless you want to be alone by that time." Isabella laughed at the funny look on her friend's face.

"I won't be alone. We'll be with Thomas, right?"

"Oh. Right." There was that pit in Isabella's stomach

again. "Well, who knows what Thomas and his new girlfriend will be doing, but I'm sure you'll have loads of new friends by then too."

"Bella, don't be silly. I'm only joking." Jemma reached over and squeezed her friend's hand. "And I'd love to go with you, if you feel like you'd like some moral support. But I do think that's when I'm supposed to be meeting my family in London. Mom has some big fashion show there and it's around Thanksgiving, I think."

Jemma's mom, Blu Foster, was a big deal in the world of design and fashion. They'd already met in Rome for a show since the girls had left Tuscany a few months ago. Now, Isabella remembered Blu giving the girls the dates in November.

"Oh, that's right. Maybe I should change the plan with Lucas. I'm sure it would be okay—"

"—Don't be silly. Of course you'll go. There'll be plenty of fashion shows to go to, and Mom would not want you to change your plan. You'll go, you'll meet your father and your sister, and then we'll have the most wonderful reunion back at the villa with everyone, if not before Christmas."

Isabella smiled. "It's funny, isn't it? How quickly things can change? I mean, I still can't get over everything that's happened—how much my life has changed since the day I found out about Arianna. I feel like I'm a completely different person, you know?"

"Do you feel like the changes have been for the

better?"

Isabella didn't even have to think about the question. She knew the changes had been for the best. She knew that she was living a life that was less stressful and much more authentic in what she felt was the way she wanted to be living. There was no doubt about that in her mind. "Oh, definitely for the better." She grinned.

"Well, I know how much that would have pleased your mom. I was so young when she died, but everyone—the whole family—has always talked about how much she loved you and what she wanted for you. It's really pretty awesome, isn't it? Especially that you've turned out to be one of my very best friends in the entire world." Jemma leaned over and gave Isabella a big hug.

"I agree with that statement. One hundred percent. I don't know how I've managed so many years without having a best girlfriend." Isabella laughed.

"Well, from what I can tell, it seems like Thomas managed to fill that roll. *But* I'm here now." Jemma laughed and got up from the table. "I'm going to start one more painting while I'm still in the mood. Are you going to write?"

"Yep. I'll be in in two minutes. Wanna coffee refill?"

Jemma grinned and handed her the cup from the table. "Yes, please. Oh, I almost forgot. I'm meeting the girls for breakfast at nine-thirty. Please say you'll come?"

"No, sorry. I would do it, actually, but Thomas and I are chatting at nine." She could tell by the look on

Jemma's face that she was disappointed, and really she *had* been saying no way more than she'd been saying yes to her friend these last few days. "But I'm sure our chat won't go long, so how bout if I meet you there when I'm done?"

Jemma smiled. "Really? Yes! And maybe we can do a bit of shopping after. I still want to show you that little market I found the other day."

"Great, sounds like a plan."

PAULA KAY

CHAPTER 5

Isabella dusted her face with a bit of powder and painted her lips with a neutral lip gloss. It was the only make-up she was wearing these days except for the coat of mascara she added on the nights that she did go out with Jemma. She laughed out loud as she readied her computer for the call with Thomas, unsure why she was even going to the trouble. Thomas had seen her without make-up hundreds of times.

She waited for Thomas to pick up the call, anxiously watching the screen of her laptop.

Finally the connection was made and a few seconds later her best friend's face appeared, hair looking disheveled per normal and more stubble on his face than she'd ever seen before. Jemma's words from the day before flashed in her mind. Thomas *was* good-looking—more handsome than she'd noticed before. She pushed the thought aside and grinned widely into the camera.

"Thomas. It's so good to see you."

"And you, my darling. Did you put a little lip gloss on for me?" Thomas laughed and Isabella could feel the warmth in her face.

"Yeah, well, I'm meeting Jemma and some girls for breakfast after this, so don't flatter yourself too much." She laughed too.

"Point taken. So how are you? Tell me everything?"

Thomas sank back into a plush-looking sofa, raising a coffee mug to his lips. Jemma's eyes did a quick sweep of the room behind him and she felt her forehead crinkle in confusion.

"Hey, did you switch hotels? It looks different."

There was no mistaking the blush on Thomas's face or how awkward he looked before responding to Isabella's question.

"Yeah, so I moved out of the hotel. I'm staying with Natasha for now."

Natasha. It was the first time Isabella had heard him say her name. He was living with her? How odd. It wasn't like Thomas to jump into something so fast with a girl. He did date a lot, but usually there was something or other that didn't work out. Then again, he was in travel mode—away from home—so maybe it wasn't really about more than convenience. Not that Thomas couldn't afford a nice hotel or apartment. His parents had given him more than enough money for his travels abroad, enough to be living at least as well as Isabella and Jemma were able to.

Isabella tried to hide the surprise that she was sure would be apparent on her face as she answered Thomas.

"Oh, really? So that sounds kinda serious. Is there something you're not telling me?" She tried to keep her voice light as per their typical bantering, but it was hard to imagine that they'd come to a place where Thomas hadn't told her something so important. They'd always told one another everything, and it made Isabella sad to think about him keeping something from her.

"Oh, well—No, not really Iz. I mean, it just happened. We just decided to try it for the next month. It seemed silly keeping the hotel when we've been spending so much time together and Natasha lives in a great neighborhood, so—well, it just made sense. But you know. Who knows what will happen, right? You know me."

There was that look that Isabella knew so well. When she saw it, her heart started to slow from its faster than normal beating. She didn't want Thomas to have a girlfriend right now—not when they were just getting ready to finally spend several months together. That was the hard, honest truth. She wanted her best friend that she hadn't seen for several months. She tried to pull herself together again, wishing that they'd not chosen to do a video chat that morning. Thomas could always tell when something was wrong with Isabella. He said he could read her face as well as his own when he looked in the mirror.

"Iz? Don't worry. Nothing's gonna change our plans, okay? I still can't wait to see you, goofball."

Isabella laughed and everything seemed normal between them once again. She took a deep breath, careful to not make it obvious on the camera as she did so. "Well, I'm sure I'll like Natasha if you like her so much. So, is she there? I should meet her."

"No. She just left. She works kinda crazy hours. She's an investment banker."

"Really? Wow. Thomas, how old is Natasha?"

There was no mistaking the blush that quickly rose to Thomas's cheeks. "Well, she is older."

"How much older? Spill it." Isabella laughed but inside she was preparing herself for the answer. She didn't want Natasha to be anything older than the twenty-somethings that Thomas typically dated. An older woman would be more serious, and that thought caused an ache in Isabella's stomach.

"She's thirty-three, Iz. Okay? She's from London, has a very good career, and for some crazy reason she seems to like me quite a lot." He laughed and Isabella guessed that he desperately wanted to change the subject. "You'll meet her soon enough, and I really hope you two like one another. Now, can we talk about you, my love?"

Isabella grinned back at him. Thomas was forever being goofy with her with his silly terms of endearment and she'd missed his daily teasing. He'd always been there to lift her up when she was feeling down or unsure of herself. Thomas had been her biggest cheerleader since the day they'd met in the fifth grade.

"Okay, okay. You're off the hook for now, but don't think that I don't want to hear more about what's going on between you and Natasha."

"Deal. We'll talk more about it later—maybe when I have a better idea of what's actually going on myself."

There it was. That made Isabella feel better all of a sudden. It wasn't serious. Thomas was just having some fun with the older woman he'd met who happened to be some glamorous British businesswoman from London. She'd have her Thomas back in no time and things would be normal once again. *Her Thomas.* She giggled, thankful that she was the only witness to the crazy thoughts in her head.

"Iz? What's so funny? And what the heck is going on with you? Let's talk about you now. You look great, by the way."

"Thanks. And nothing's funny. And yes, I do have some news, actually."

"Yeah, what you were texting me about last night. What's up? I've been wondering what it is you have to tell me."

"You know how I've been talking with my birth father these past months—with Lucas?"

"Yeah. And I think that's awesome—and slightly unbelievable—in a good way, of course."

"Well, it looks like we're finally going to meet in person. He invited me to come there—to go to San Francisco—for Thanksgiving."

"Wow, that's great, Iz. And your parents? What do Emily and Richard think about this plan?" Thomas winked as he asked the question, and Isabella felt that grateful feeling that she'd had toward her parents ever since they'd showed such amazing support for her travel plans, something that still slightly shocked her.

"Well, now that you mention it, I guess I've not told them yet. But I don't have plans with them until Christmas anyway. They're planning to come to the villa." As the words left her lips, Isabella remembered that she hadn't officially invited Thomas for Christmas yet and she really wanted him to come. Given their conversation so far—about Natasha and London—she felt she'd do better to wait to invite him in person. He knew how much she wanted to introduce him to everyone—to her new wonderful extended family; she'd practically put money on the fact that he'd say yes. But she'd wait for that for now.

"It does sound like your parents have been handling everything so well—incredibly well, really. I mean, who knew that they'd be so supportive of you doing things that didn't include your dreams of going to Harvard. I'm still shocked by it all, if I'm being honest."

"You're not kidding. I've been shocked too, but ever since I found out about Arianna, they've done nothing but give me their support. And really, Thomas—they love the vineyard, my grandparents, and everyone just as much as I do. Those Italians sure do know how to make one feel welcome."

"So I've heard. I can't wait to get to Italy myself. And of course I do want to meet your family soon too."

There it was—the perfect opportunity to bring up Christmas. How could she not bring it up?

"So, about meeting my family. Funny you should say." Isabella laughed. "Thomas, I want to invite you for Christmas—at the villa. It will be so lovely and you'll be able to meet everyone then—well, aside from Lucas, but I'm sure that we'll work on getting him out there too at some point soon. Say you'll come."

Thomas looked noticeably uncomfortable as Isabella waited for his answer to her invitation.

"We'll see, okay, Iz? Thanks for the invitation. Of course, I'd love to come—I can't wait to meet your family. I—I just have to see how things go here, so can we talk about it again later?"

Isabella's heart plummeted again. She didn't remember a conversation between her and Thomas ever making her feel so emotional, and she hated it.

"Okay. Sure. We can talk about it later. And on that note, I better run. I don't wanna keep Jemma and the others waiting too long." Isabella made herself smile into the camera.

"Iz? Are you mad at me? Don't be mad, okay?"

"No. No, not at all. Promise." She smiled again, but she really felt like crying. She wasn't mad but she was feeling hurt. Something was changing between her and

Thomas, and she had a strong suspicion that that something was Natasha. At least she had some time to mentally prepare herself for it before she saw them together in a few weeks. She'd be ready for it by then.

"Okay. Good. Iz?"

"Yeah?"

"I miss you like crazy and I can't wait to see you."

Isabella smiled and it wasn't forced at all this time. "I miss you too. Chat next week? Normal time?"

"It's a date. Enjoy your breakfast."

"Thanks. Have a good day, Thomas."

Isabella clicked the button that ended their conversation and stared at her computer screen for a few minutes, trying to process how she was feeling about the conversation that they'd just had. It wasn't like her to feel jealous—if that was even the right word to describe the way she was feeling. She sighed.

Everything was going to be fine. Her friendship with Thomas was going to be fine, and as long as this Natasha was a nice woman, she'd have to learn to just be happy for Thomas when it came to his relationships. They weren't kids any more, so sooner or later it was going to happen for both of them. And besides, deep down in her heart, she really did suspect that Natasha wasn't going to be in the picture for long. That was the thought that she'd be hanging on to for now—even if it was kind of twisted in a way.

CHAPTER 6

Isabella looked around the table at the small group of women who seemed to be enjoying their food and the lively conversation that was going on at the typical Parisian cafe. It was a beautiful morning and the tables outside were crowded with families, friends, and couples. Isabella plastered a smile on her face, but it wasn't where she wanted to be in that moment.

She smiled at Jemma sitting next to her as her friend reached over to put her hand on Isabella's arm and whispered to her.

"Hey, are you okay? You seem pretty quiet."

"Yeah. Yeah, I'm fine."

"Are you sure? Bella, you're not fine. I can tell. Was it your call with Thomas?"

"Maybe. Oh, I don't know. Everything will be fine. I don't wanna think about it right now." Isabella looked up as the waiter set her drink down in front of her, happy for the slight distraction. Jemma's eyes were still on her as she took a sip of her drink. "Jem, I'm fine. Can we talk about it later? Please?"

Jemma gave Isabella's arm a slight squeeze. "Yes, of course. I'm sorry."

"Don't be sorry. It's fine. Really."

Isabella tried to be cheerful throughout the rest of breakfast, but the truth was that she was very thankful when it was time for her and Jemma to say goodbye to the other women. She did need to talk to her friend about what had her feeling so strange. Jemma would help her to feel better about things. She seemed to have that effect on her.

"Okay, so I'm kinda guessing that you're not up for shopping?"

Isabella gave her friend a quick hug. "Do you mind? I'm just really not in the mood. But I do want to talk. Maybe we can go for a walk in the park?"

Their apartment was only a few blocks from a gorgeous park that the two loved to sit in a few days a week. Jemma would paint there, and Isabella had found a quiet table under a tree that was very conducive to her writing. It had become one of their favorite spots in Paris.

"Of course." Jemma laughed. "It'll give me a chance to work off some of that big breakfast I just ate."

They walked the four blocks to the park in comfortable silence. Isabella had grown to appreciate this about their friendship—she never felt any judgment from Jemma and she knew that she could trust her with anything. It was a new thing for her—having such a strong connection with another girl. Finally she knew what she'd been missing all those years in high school, not having a best girlfriend—not that she'd imagined any other friendship could ever take the place of the one she'd always had with Thomas.

Thomas. Just thinking about him made her stomach tug. What was wrong with her? It was probably nothing—this weird sinking feeling she'd had ever since their conversation had ended earlier.

"So, what's up?"

Isabella looked up at her friend's voice, wondering if she could even begin to verbalize what she wasn't even sure she was feeling. It was always best to just blurt things out with Jemma. She was that kind of girl—no nonsense, get right to the point.

"So, apparently this girl Thomas mentioned last week—"

"The London girl?"

Isabella nodded. "Yeah, so in actuality she's not a girl at all—in fact, she's thirty-three—and Thomas is living with her all of a sudden. Oh, and she has a name—Natasha." Isabella hated the way the name sounded coming out of her mouth. She stopped on the footpath and then turned to walk over to one of the benches, Jemma following behind her.

"Hm."

"What's hm?" Isabella was trying not to cry. She

refused to be that emotional about the whole silly thing.

"Why do you think you're so upset about it?"

"Oh, I dunno, Jem. I mean, Thomas can date whomever he wants. I've never said anything about the girls he dates. And believe me, there's been quite a few."

"Okay, so what feels different about this? Are you sure you don't have feelings for him? I know we've joked about it—talked about it before—and you always deny it, but I dunno—"

Isabella was shaking her head. "No. No, I don't think that's it."

"You don't *think* that's it? Come on, Bella."

"No. I mean, he's like a brother to me. If anything— if there's any jealousy there, I think it's just that I haven't seen him for a while. I miss him. And I guess if I'm being honest, I don't wanna share him when we get to London. Does that make sense?"

Jemma reached over to pull Isabella in for a hug. "It does make sense."

Isabella pulled away and wiped at a few tears that had somehow escaped down her cheeks, even though she'd been trying desperately not to get so emotional. She sniffled. "Ack. I don't know why I'm crying right now. It's really not that big of a deal, is it?"

Jemma smiled. "I think you're just feeling kinda stressed—with the book, probably with me on your case about not having enough fun." She laughed lightly. "You probably just need to let out some emotions in general, ya know?"

"You do make a good point."

Isabella had become much more self aware and much better about expressing herself since she'd left her home in Connecticut months ago, but holding in her feelings and her stress was an old habit that she'd probably need to keep working on for a while. Jemma was a great role model in that regard.

"So, wanna hear my idea?"

Jemma was grinning when Isabella looked over at her. "Sure."

"I say we go by the corner shop, get a pint of that lovely home-made ice cream that you love so much, and then go rent sad French movies at the movie shop down the road. What do you say? Can you take a little time off today? I'll even be in charge of building the fire."

"Sad movies? Why not something funny maybe?"

Jemma shrugged. "You know—so you have a reason to cry."

Isabella laughed, incredibly thankful for this friendship that she'd found so unexpectedly. Jemma always seemed to know the right things to do and say to cheer her up.

"That sounds like a marvelous plan. What would I ever do without you?"

Jemma didn't miss a beat in her reply. "Sit in front of your computer every day—all day—writing books based on all the angst and desperation you're feeling because you have no best friend to talk it over with and ending your life is not an option because you're becoming the most famous author who ever lived." Jemma stopped to finally take a breath and Isabella burst out laughing, already feeling so much better than she ever would have imagined a few hours earlier.

CHAPTER 7

Isabella stood up from tying her sneakers just as Jemma entered the living room. She zipped her hoodie up and grabbed her favorite light blue stocking cap from the hall closet.

"Hey. Morning." Jemma yawned. "Where are you off to so early?"

"Morning. I can't believe it's our last full day here in Paris. I don't know what I was thinking. The time really got away from me the last few weeks."

"I know what you mean. I'm excited about London, but Paris—well, it's Paris, right?" Jemma laughed. "I really do love it here. So, where are you off to? And do you want company?"

Isabella bit her bottom lip. She didn't want to hurt Jemma's feelings—she should have gone with her to the Eiffel Tower weeks ago when she'd asked her to go. But today was just for her. It had to be that way.

Jemma understood. They'd talked about it before—at the first location they'd been to in Italy—the first location that had been on Arianna's map after Tuscany. That was when she'd started it all. She gestured toward the table in response to Jemma's question.

Jemma's eyes followed Isabella's until they landed on the object that sat wrapped up on the table, before Isabella crossed the room to pick it up and tuck it into the small purse around her shoulder.

"Oh. I didn't realize that you'd not done that here yet. So, the Eiffel Tower?"

Isabella nodded

"It's perfect, Bella. The view is amazing and you're getting there early, so there won't be many tourists. You should be able to find a quiet spot—at least for a few minutes." Jemma took a step toward her, wrapping her arms around her neck in a quick hug. "Just don't get arrested." She whispered in her ear, giggling.

"You know me—I'll be discreet as always." Isabella smiled back at her friend before she walked out the door.

"Hey, wait."

Isabella pushed the door back open before she'd had a chance to shut it tight, sticking her head back into the apartment.

"You forgot this." Jemma handed her the leather journal that she'd left lying on the table in her rush to get going.

"Oh, thanks, Jem. I won't be late."

Isabella pulled her stocking cap on as soon as she

stepped out into the cool early morning air. She walked quickly, thinking about how her last few weeks in Paris had been. She'd worked pretty much nonstop, determined to get her book in before the date she'd set with her editor. E-mailing it off to her the day before had felt extremely rewarding, and she'd celebrated by taking Jemma out to a very expensive dinner.

Today was about ending her time in Paris well, and this morning was all about her mother. She held the journal tightly to her chest as she thought about Arianna and Arianna's letters to her. Isabella wondered how her birth mother would have spent her time in Paris, and the thought brought a sudden rush of regret. She had been missing too much of the trip. Jemma was right about that.

She tried to brush the thought aside. She was mostly done with the book now. It was time to focus on having some good times with her best friends.

Thomas. She smiled merely thinking about seeing him again after so many weeks had gone by. She'd worked hard to calm her feelings of jealously and for the most part had decided to look forward to seeing him without any worry as to how it would all unfold. She'd cross that bridge later, if and when things seemed any different between them. But she had to have faith in a friendship that really had stood the test of time all these years. And besides, knowing Thomas, things with Natasha probably weren't as serious as she'd imagined them to be.

Isabella looked up to see the Eiffel Tower and a line

of people waiting for their turn in the elevator, which, by a quick glance at the time, she guessed had only just begun taking visitors up the structure. She debated waiting with the other tourists, but then decided to walk the stairs to the first level, which she thought might be less crowded than the other platforms. She needed a little exercise anyway, having spent so much time at her computer the last few weeks.

Climbing the stairs felt great. The air still held a bit of a chill—perfect weather for getting a little exercise. She was virtually alone for most of the ascent, taking her time to peer out at the city below. She climbed the last steps before entering onto the first-floor platform. There were a few other people, but it seemed like she was right in assuming that most would be journeying higher up the structure.

Isabella walked around the outside of the platform, taking in the views of the city from every angle. How lucky was she? She knew that no matter how distracted she became by her writing or whatever else was going on in her life, she had to remind herself of everything that she'd been given.

Paris. She'd just spent almost an entire month in a beautiful apartment in the heart of the city that people dreamed of visiting. Arianna couldn't possibly have imagined that Isabella would grow up dreaming about the very places that her own birth mother had longed to see and experience.

Isabella looked around the platform, before crossing it to a spot that was relatively clear of tourists. She sat cross-legged and opened the journal. She read the first letter from Arianna and thought again about what her mother's money had done for her. She'd always be grateful for the opportunities that she now had because of all the wealth Arianna had left her.

She turned the page to read the next letter. These were the ones that she'd not shared with anyone else yet. She could almost picture Arianna writing them—just a few years older than Isabella was now. Had she been feeling well when the words were written? The letters were dated and she knew that the dates coincided with the time Arianna had been with Isabella's grandmother, Lia, in Tuscany. She wanted to think that her mother had been feeling well then—that writing the letters had made her feel better somehow.

Isabella took a deep breath in as she began to read.

PAULA KAY

CHAPTER 8

My Sweet Bella,

I've long since made peace with my death, which is coming soon. I've made peace with the fact that there are so many things I've not done, so many things I've not experienced.

We never know, do we? What the future might hold—what direction our lives might take.

So now, I only think of you, my darling daughter—of everything that I wish for you.

I have so many hopes and dreams for you, Bella. I want everything for you. But most of all I want you to be happy, to not waste time thinking about regrets or a future that is far from now.

These are the things I wish for you—that I want desperately for you.

I want you to always have hope within your heart—to know that no matter what the past holds or who you were yesterday, your future can be whatever you imagine it to be.

What are your hopes and dreams, Bella? Do you know?

Spend some time getting to know yourself, without the distractions of others, without the distractions of the things (and people) that bring you stress.

Travel. See the world if it's what you desire. Have an adventure and don't ever lose sight of that belief—of that hope—that all your dreams can come true.

I want you to become the very best version of yourself that you can be—the version of yourself that makes you happiest and leaves you feeling content and complete.

I want for you to know love, Bella—to give your heart to another for all eternity.

If I have any regrets, my biggest one is that I didn't live long enough to know the true love of my soulmate. I didn't know what it was like to have an open heart until the end of my days. I'd spent too much of my short life guarded, being afraid to let someone in who could make me feel the pain of potential loss.

Take chances with your heart when you know deep in your soul that the one looking into your eyes loves you like no other.

Be brave and courageous when it comes to love, Bella. Experience it deeply without holding back.

Lastly (although there are too many things for words that I want for you)—lastly, I want for you to know a sense of family, a true sense of home.

I didn't really know this for myself until the end, and then it was the most important thing of all to me. If I have one wish, one prayer for you above all others, it's this—that you would be surrounded by people who love you, who you can depend on and who you call family. I dare to imagine that by now, my family—our family—has also become yours, Bella. I want you to always have a safe place to land—to always have your family and your place to come home to…whatever that looks like for you.

I'd by lying if I said that my heart is not breaking for everything that I will miss in never getting to hold you in my arms once again.

But these things make me smile—imagining you, my sweet girl—filled with hope, being loved, and knowing the peace and contentment that comes from having a home that is filled with a family that loves and supports you until the end of time.

I know that you will have these things. You deserve everything good and more.

When you think of me, as you read these letters or look at pictures of me, please don't be sad.

Smile now, live your life well, and be happy always.

I love you, my sweet Bella.

Your Mother,
Arianna Sinclair

Isabella wiped at just the hint of a tear making its way down her cheek. She'd read the letters—the entire journal—too many times to count, but it was rare that not one tear fell from her eyes. It was the kind of letter that needed to be read over and over—especially for someone as headstrong and hard on herself as she was. She knew that much was true.

It was interesting to think about the things that her

mother had wanted for her. She was young. She had so much time to figure out what she wanted in life—time to feel the sort of happiness and contentment that Arianna had wanted for her. She realized, even as she was having the thought, how ridiculous it was. Arianna probably had thought that she'd had all the time in the world too.

Isabella sighed as she stood up from where she'd been sitting away from the other tourists. She did need to figure some things out, to let go a little more. She definitely needed to make a commitment to herself about enjoying this next leg of her trip with Jemma and Thomas. She'd do that much in honor of her mother's wishes for her—she owed her that much.

She made her way to the elevator to take it to the top. She felt tired all of a sudden, and walking the remaining steps to the next landing was not as appealing. She had one thing left to do before she left Paris, and she wanted the very best view of the city when she did it.

Isabella stepped out of the elevator, thankful that for some odd reason it wasn't as crowded on the higher-level platform as she'd thought it would be. She made her way to the outermost walkway, her hand tightening instinctively on her purse. Ever since she'd received the box of items from her birth mother—ever since her grandmother had showed her Arianna's map and given her the small urn of ashes—Isabella had had the idea of what she had to do with her mother's ashes.

Jemma had played devil's advocate, when Isabella had shared her plan to spread the ashes in the places that they'd be traveling too. She knew there was a risk—that it wasn't exactly legal in most places, including from the top of the Eiffel Tower, but it wasn't more than a pinch or so in each place. Isabella was willing to take that risk for the sake of doing something meaningful in honor of Arianna—it was her way of taking the trip with her mother, as odd as it sounded when she'd first told the idea to Jemma.

Now it had become a ritual of sorts—one that she looked forward to as a way to transition from place to place on the journey that she was on. It was her journey, but it was Arianna's also.

Isabella smiled as she reached into her bag to take the top off of the small urn. Inside the ashes were already divided into very small plastic bags that she could discreetly take out one by one. She did so now, opening one and walking to a place where she felt comfortable regarding the lack of wind and people close by.

"Bon voyage. Thank you for Paris." she whispered as the ashes left the bag.

PAULA KAY

CHAPTER 9

Isabella stood back to look at the map on the wall, before taking it down to pack. She'd just highlighted Paris in green, which now matched all of the locations that Arianna had marked in Italy—all of the places Isabella and Jemma had been to prior to landing in Paris weeks ago.

It had been nice to stay put for a while in Paris. The moving around so quickly had been fun but a bit hectic when it came to her writing. Somehow she'd managed it, though. She still couldn't believe that she'd actually written her first novel in such a short time. Somehow the words had just flowed. Well, she had yet to get the manuscript back from the editor she'd hired but she wouldn't dwell on the revision process just yet. She was still basking in the feeling of accomplishment for having completed it.

"Bella, are you looking forward to Ireland?" Jemma had come over beside her to peer at the map. "And is Thomas going to join us for that?"

"Yes, I'm looking forward to it, and in answer to your

question about Thomas—I guess I don't really know. I mean, he's been saying that he's coming, but I think I need to prepare for the fact that he might change his mind—you know, now that Natasha's in the picture." Isabella shook her head as if doing so would shake the thoughts away. "I don't know. I don't want to think about that right now. I guess we'll just wait and see."

"Well, we've got a few weeks in London anyway. I can't wait to show you everything—I'm sure Thomas and *Natahhhhsha* will have plenty to show us too, but I've always loved London since the first time my mother took me there as a little girl. I wanna show you all the things I love about it."

Isabella laughed. Jemma was being funny in regards to Natasha, and she should be worried that the poor girl wouldn't be getting a fair chance from either of them. "Jem, let's not be too hard on Thomas's girlfriend, okay? I don't want my weird feelings to color what you might think about her. And yes, I want you to show me absolutely everything. I can't wait."

Jemma laughed too. "I know. I'm only joking." She looked around the room. "So, I'm about done with my packing. How 'bout you?"

Isabella carefully took the map off the wall and began to roll it up to fit in the cylinder-shaped container they'd picked up for it. "Yep, this is it for me too, I guess. One last walk in the park, followed by Nutella crepes and a coffee?"

Jemma grinned. "It's as if you can read my mind, *ma chérie*."

Isabella tried to calm her nerves as they waited for the plane to come to its complete stop. The morning commute to the airport had been uneventful, followed by a very short flight to what would be Isabella's third county now on her travels abroad. Unlike the first flight she'd taken, from the U.S. to Florence, this time her nervousness did not have to do with flying at all. She was beyond nervous about seeing Thomas and it was really starting to bother her.

Jemma seemed to be watching her intently as she took her phone out from her purse to turn it on.

"You okay? Everything's gonna be fine. You'll see. And I can't wait to meet Thomas."

Isabella took a deep breath as she punched in the text to let Thomas know that they were on the ground. "What? Sorry. Why am I feeling so weird? And I'm anxious for you to meet him also." She smiled at Jemma as the line of people started making their way down the aisle, just as her phone beeped with a text.

I'm here. Just outside of baggage. Can't wait to see you, Iz!

"Well?" Jemma was waiting for her to say something.

"He's here. Says he'll meet us outside of baggage claim."

They reached up to collect their bags from the

overhead compartment, and Isabella thought she might throw up as she made her way to the door.

They cleared passport control rather quickly, and in no time at all they were waiting for their bags to show up on the carousel. Isabella was trying to take deep breaths to slow her heart rate as they waited in line to go through customs with their bags. The line was moving quickly. Thomas was just on the other side of the doors waiting for her. Why was she so darn nervous?

Jemma looked back at her as she waited for Isabella to come through. "Ready?"

Isabella grinned at her, remembering how excited she was to see Thomas—to see her best friend. She was being ridiculous for feeling so nervous. "Yes, I can't wait for you to meet him. I can't wait to see him." She picked up the pace and felt a renewed sense of excitement, the nerves replaced by the typical sense of familiarity she always felt around Thomas.

Then she saw him before he saw her. He was looking at the tall beautiful woman by his side—a woman who could only be Natasha—with her head thrown back, laughing at something being said between them. He was looking at her in a way that made Isabella's heart sink, but she plastered a big grin on her face just as Thomas looked up to notice her walking toward him.

CHAPTER 10

"Izzy!"

Isabella laughed as Thomas picked her up off the ground, plastering her cheeks with kisses.

"It's so good to see you." He was grinning at her when he finally put her down.

Isabella reached for his neck to hug him close. "I've missed you so much," she whispered in his ear, noticing Jemma grinning nearby. With one last squeeze she let him go. "Thomas, this is Jemma. I've been dying for you two to meet. I can't believe it's finally happening."

"Ah, the famous Jemma—lovely as I remember from our video introduction." He leaned over to give her a hug.

Isabella noticed the woman—presumably Natasha—put her hand on Thomas's back just as he'd finished hugging Jemma.

"Honey, are you going to introduce me?" She laughed lightly but Isabella didn't miss the expression on her face. Was it one of amusement or annoyance?

Thomas took the woman's hand. "Yes, of course, darling." He turned toward Isabella. "This is Natasha. Natasha, meet my best friend, Isabella."

Natasha stuck out her hand to grasp Isabella's in a firm handshake. "It's great to finally meet you, Isabella. Thomas has told me a lot about you."

That's funny, because he's hardly told me anything about you.

Isabella smiled. "It's nice to finally meet you also."

Jemma stuck her hand out toward Natasha. "Hi, I'm Jemma. Thanks for meeting us at the airport. That was really great of you."

"Of course. We've got a car waiting and we'll have the driver drop you two at your apartment," said Natasha.

"And you'll come in? To hang out for a while, yes?" said Isabella, directing her question toward Thomas.

She saw the quick glance between him and Natasha. "Of course. I'd love to. I'm afraid Natasha has to be getting back to work—"

Isabella didn't miss the squeeze of Natasha's hand as Thomas directed his next words to her.

"—Honey, you don't mind if I go to help them get settled, do you?"

Isabella hated watching the exchange. It looked odd—Thomas asking for permission to spend time with Isabella. She watched Natasha's face intently as she responded, her expression not quite matching her words.

"No, you go right ahead. I'm sure you two have a lot of catching up to do. Let's get going, shall we then?"

Isabella tried to focus on the chatter between Thomas and Jemma as they pointed at things out the window on the way to the apartment, but her attention kept shifting to Natasha, who was quietly looking out the window.

She didn't seem like the type of woman Thomas would date at all. She was very well put together, dressed in a business suit, her dark hair pulled back in a bun with not a hair out of place. It wasn't that she wasn't pretty. She was, but something about her was off-putting to Isabella. She tried to shake the feeling, wanting to like her. She had to try—for Thomas.

"Here we are." Natasha finally turned toward the group in the car as they pulled up next to a very cool South Bank apartment building.

Isabella and Jemma had found the apartment online and deemed it perfect for them as soon as they saw the pictures of the view. Thomas had gone ahead to check it out and he'd already collected the keys for them the day before.

Isabella turned to Jemma as they waited for the driver to help get their bags out of the car. "Jem, this looks pretty great, huh?"

"I already love the neighborhood. Look how cute everything looks."

Isabella heard Natasha's laugh as she got out of the car to stand next to them. "Well, I don't know if cute is quite the right word to describe one of London's better neighborhoods, but I'm glad you like it."

Maybe she didn't mean to come off as snooty, but her accent probably wasn't helping with the impression she was delivering, Isabella thought as Jemma stuck her tongue out toward Natasha's back. She turned toward Natasha. "Are you sure you can't come up for a little bit?"

"No, thanks for asking." Natasha looked at her watch. "Actually, I really do have to run. I've got a meeting in an hour. But it was lovely meeting you both. Isabella, would you like to have coffee sometime in the next few days?"

Isabella hoped her smiled seemed genuine. Natasha's invitation surprised her, but it made sense that they should get to know one another. She nodded in response to Natasha's question. "Sure. I'd love to. Do you want to text me with the time and place?"

"Sounds good. I can get your number from Thomas."

Natasha turned back around toward Thomas, planting a big kiss squarely on his lips. "I'll be home late tonight, so don't wait for me for dinner."

"Okay, honey. I hope your meeting goes well."

"Don't have too much fun without me." She laughed as she got back into the car.

Thomas leaned down to give her a quick kiss, laughing also. "I won't. I'll just help to get the girls settled and take them for some food."

"Okay, but seriously, Thomas, be home before seven."

Natasha had spoken the last statement quietly but

Isabella and Jemma had been standing near enough to hear it.

Jemma turned to Isabella and rolled her eyes.

Isabella turned away from the car, feeling like she was invading their privacy standing so close—hearing things that she was pretty sure would embarrass Thomas. It was odd to think about Thomas being with someone who was giving him a curfew. She sighed, feeling like this was going to be an odd four weeks with her best friend—not at all how she'd pictured it in her head when they'd planned it a few months earlier—before Natasha was in the picture.

She shook her head, as if doing so could shake the bad thoughts she was already having about Thomas's new girlfriend. She'd have to give her a chance. What choice did she have? The coffee invitation had been thoughtful, and maybe her impression would change after she and Natasha had a chance to sit down and talk—just the two of them.

Before she could think about it any more, Thomas had grabbed the two large suitcases and started toward the front door of the building.

"Well, come on, you two. Let's get you settled."

Isabella and Jemma followed, Jemma eyeing Thomas's muscles and then turning toward Isabella mouthing the words "nice body", causing both of them to burst into laughter.

Thomas turned toward them with a big grin on his

face. "What's so funny?" He pulled Isabella close with his arm around her waist. "You laughing at me?"

"Never!" Isabella giggled. "Go on. Let us in."

Thomas took the key out of his pocket and opened the door. "After you, ladies."

Isabella and Jemma stepped through the door and walked straight across to the expansive open living room. There were wall-to-ceiling windows, and a spectacular view of the River Thames and the city beyond it.

"I must say, you did do a really great job finding the place. The view's wonderful and you're only a block or so from the Waterloo tube station. You'll be able to get around the city easily."

"And how far are you from here?"

Isabella was glad that Jemma had asked the question that was also on her mind. How much of Thomas would she be seeing?

"Not too far. I'd say about fifteen minutes by tube," said Thomas.

"So just far enough away so that you don't get too sick of seeing me, huh?" Isabella grinned at him and he walked over to give her a big hug.

"Bite your tongue, silly girl. I could never get sick of this face." He squeezed her cheeks together gently with his fingers and then leaned forward to kiss the tip of her nose. He turned toward Jemma with his arm around Isabella's waist. "She's pretty wonderful, don't you think?"

Jemma grinned and nodded in response.

He said, "A bit annoying at times, but wonderful all the same."

Isabella punched him on the arm.

"Ow!" He grinned at her. "Well, you can be."

"Yeah, okay. Well you haven't been around me in a quite a long time, so we'll see about that," said Isabella.

She was aware that Thomas was looking at her very intently. Something felt different between them—not really good or bad; maybe it was that she really had changed since they'd last been together.

"Yes, we shall see." Thomas winked at her and then made his way back to where he'd left the suitcases in the hall. "Let's get your stuff situated in the bedrooms. Who's going where?"

"You take the master, Bella."

"Are you sure? I had the bigger bedroom in Paris. You can have it."

Jemma was poking her head in the bigger of the two bedrooms. "No, you take it. There's a nice desk in here and I figure you're going to want to get back to your writing. The other one is just as nice and I can set my easel up in the living room near the window, if you don't mind."

"Sounds pretty perfect to me."

Thomas was watching them and laughing.

"What?" asked Isabella.

"Oh, nothing. It just seems that you two really have

your travel routine down, don't you—getting settled in—who goes where? You're the travel duo that was made for one another."

Isabella looked at Jemma and grinned. "Yeah, I guess it really has been working out very well. Jem's a dream to travel with."

"As are you, my dear."

Isabella turned her attention toward Thomas. "And we hope that we're going to be looking at three bedroom places for Dublin? You've not said anything about it for awhile."

Thomas visibly cringed. "Yeah, I guess we'll need to talk about that. But not now. Now, I'm thinking you two might like for me to treat you to a nice pub meal?"

Isabella winked at Jemma. "Okay, I guess he's off the hook for now, because I'm starving and all I've been thinking about is some delicious fish and chips."

"Sounds like a plan to me," said Jemma.

"Great! So, let's go check out this new neighborhood of yours," said Thomas.

CHAPTER 11

Isabella swallowed the big bite of fish that was in her mouth as she scooped up some fries. "Oh, wow. I've possibly never been this satisfied with a meal in all my life."

Jemma laughed. "That hungry, huh? I know. I'm hungry too and it is very good."

"I'm going to eat all the fish and chips while we're here. Oh, and possibly all the bangers and mash too." Isabella laughed and then noticed Thomas looking at her with an amused expression on his face. "Thomas, what? You keep staring at me like I've grown another head or something. It's making me feel slightly self-conscious."

"Don't feel self-conscious. Quite the contrary, I'd say."

"What? What exactly do you mean by that?" Isabella noticed that Jemma was now the one watching the conversation with an amused expression on her face.

"Well, I've just never seen you quite like this—eating like this, I mean."

"You're crazy! Have you forgotten all of our diner binges? Double fries with chili?" Isabella laughed and then turned to Jemma. "Thomas and I practically lived in this diner back home. It was our favorite hangout spot…" She stopped for a moment, looking at Thomas. "Well, apart from hanging out at Thomas's house, which I loved even more. But anyway, I'm not sure what you're talking about, mister."

"Yeah, but you forget. Most of the time you were in training for the track team, so it wasn't always the double doubles for you." He turned to Jemma. "It was more typical for our friend here to be ordering double servings of salad—"

"—with chicken. It's not like I was starving myself or anything." Isabella punched Thomas lightly on the arm. "I don't miss that training—not at all." She put her hand on her stomach and then cringed. "Although, I guess maybe I should start cutting back a bit. I have gained at least ten pounds. Thank you very much for noticing." She laughed as she spoke, but she was now wondering if Thomas was really taking about the fact that she'd put on weight. Now that she'd had the thought, she swore Thomas was eyeing her stomach.

"Isabella Dawson, are you crazy?" Thomas leaned in to put his arm around her and then kissed her quickly on the cheek. "I *am* talking about the fact that you've put on a few pounds and I think you look amazing—absolutely more gorgeous than I've ever seen you."

Now she was having a hard time looking him in the eye as she felt her face grow warm.

"Iz, look at me."

He was laughing and she needed to make light of the conversation.

She looked up at him, plastering a goofy grin on her face. "Okay, you're embarrassing me now."

Thomas smiled back at her, and she wasn't exactly sure why the intense look in his eyes was making her stomach do flip-flops all of the sudden. It was just Thomas, being silly as usual.

"I'm serious, Iz. You look really beautiful—and happy. Very happy."

"I am happy." Isabella caught Jemma's eye across the table as Thomas focused back on his food for a few seconds. Jemma was smiling as she mouthed the words "we need to talk" to Isabella.

Isabella noticed that Thomas had started to check the time on his phone every so often; checking her own, she saw that it was getting close to seven o'clock. "You need to get going, huh?"

Thomas nodded, but he didn't look happy about it. "Yeah, sorry. I promised Natasha I'd be there when she got home tonight."

Isabella nodded, biting her tongue to keep from saying something she shouldn't. "It's okay. I'm pretty wiped out myself."

"Me too. Let's get the check," said Jemma.

After fighting for a few minutes over who'd pick up the tab, Isabella and Jemma finally relented and waited for Thomas outside of the pub. It was the first time they'd had a few minutes alone together since they'd arrived, and Isabella was dying to know what Jemma's impression of Thomas was.

"So, what do you think? About Thomas?"

"Well, I think he's pretty great, but that's not all I think." She gave Isabella a look. "We have so much to talk about."

"Okay, shh. He's coming." Isabella giggled as Thomas came up between them, offering an elbow to link with each of them.

"Ladies, this has been wonderful. Thank you for allowing me the pleasure of your company. I'll walk you back to the apartment."

Jemma laughed. "You're goofy. In a good way, of course. And thanks so much for the meal. Next time, it's on me."

"Deal."

"Yeah, thanks, Thomas—for the meal, the airport pick-up, helping us get settled—"

"—Stop, Iz. You're very welcome, but you know that I couldn't wait to see you. I'm so glad you're here. Really. It feels wonderful to spend time with you."

"Well, I hope we get to see a lot more of you," said Isabella.

"True." Jemma nodded.

"Great, I'll talk to Natasha about having you over for dinner one night—or we'll all go out. But for sure, we'll have you over so you can see where we live—if you want to."

Isabella thought Thomas looked embarrassed, and it wasn't like him. What was all the fuss?

"Sure. Whatever works best for you guys," said Isabella. "And will you give Natasha my number so she can let me know about coffee?"

"Sure."

"It's okay with you, right? I mean it was her idea."

"Of course. Why wouldn't it be?"

"No reason. I figure you'd want us to get to know one another—give me a chance to okay the love of your life."

Isabella was teasing him, but Thomas didn't look very amused.

"Let's not get carried away or anything."

"Thomas, you're blushing."

"I'm not. Stop."

"You most certainly are."

They'd arrived at the apartment and Jemma was waving from up ahead. "I'm just going to go on up. Great to meet you, Thomas, and hope to see you again real soon."

Isabella guessed that she'd given her and Thomas some privacy on purpose when Natasha's name had come up in the conversation. She turned back to Thomas, who was looking at the time on his phone.

"So you are blushing and I do realize you that you need to get going, but we'll talk more about this later, yeah?"

"More about what?"

"More about you and Natasha, silly. I wanna know everything—well, okay—maybe not everything, but you know what I mean. You've been so tight-lipped about your relationship and then you spring it on me that you're living with her. I figure that means you are pretty into her, if not in love with her."

"Yeah. Yeah, I am pretty crazy about her if I'm being honest. She's unlike anyone I've ever met. So, that's the truth."

He looked at his phone again, which Isabella could see was lighting up with an incoming call. "Natasha?"

He nodded. "Sorry, Iz. I should take this." He gave her quick squeeze. "Sleep well and we'll talk tomorrow, okay?"

She nodded. "Go. Go—before you get in more trouble." She winked at him.

Isabella stood outside for a few minutes after Thomas had walked away. It had been a good afternoon, and she didn't want anything to ruin the time that they'd all had together. Seeing Thomas watch his phone so closely had her more than a bit puzzled, though. He'd never been like that with anyone he'd ever dated. Everything in his past relationships had been pretty casual. If a girl had tried to give him rules or tell him what to do, he would have backed way off of the relationship.

But they weren't kids any more, and it seemed like Thomas was in a serious grown-up relationship. Maybe it was Isabella that was the odd one. She'd never even dated all that much. She'd had boyfriends in high school, but nothing that was long-term or even the least bit serious to her. She'd really try hard with Natasha. Thomas deserved that, and she wanted to like her.

"Hey, are you coming up or what?"

Isabella jumped when she heard Jemma's voice from above her.

"Good grief. You scared me to death." She laughed. "Yeah, I'm coming right now."

"Good. I have the teakettle on. I know you're tired but we need to talk." Jemma laughed and closed the window.

Jemma set the cup of tea down on the breakfast table in front of Isabella. "So spill it."

Isabella laughed. "Spill what?"

"I wanna know what the heck is going on between you and Thomas." Jemma sat down across from her. "Because you can't convince me that there's not something besides friendship going on between the two of you. Now that I've seen you together with my own eyes."

"Oh, Jem. Don't be ridiculous. Honestly. I'm not even really sure what you're talking about."

"I'm taking about the way that he looks at you, the things he says—just the way he is with you really. Come on, Bella. You can't seriously not notice it."

Isabella shook her head. "No. Thomas always jokes with me like that. It's just the way we are with one another."

"Really? Like he's always telling you how gorgeous you are?"

Isabella felt her face go hot instantly. "Well okay. It's not like he hasn't said that to me before, but—" She didn't even want to have the thought that was in her head, let alone voice it out loud to another person. That would make it real. That would make her start thinking about things she shouldn't be thinking about.

"—But what?"

"But—okay, if I'm being completely honest, something did feel kinda different today. But he's with Natasha so honestly, Jem, I don't even think we should be talking about this."

"Mm-hm."

"Please. Or can we at least talk about it later? I'm pretty tired and I know you must be too. But you did like him, didn't you?" She felt her face light up as she asked the question. She so desperately wanted her two best friends to like one another.

Jemma was smiling. "Yes, of course. I like him a lot.

He's everything you described and more. Way more."

Isabella laughed and said goodnight, making her way to her room where she could overthink things in private.

PAULA KAY

CHAPTER 12

Isabella was rushing around the apartment trying to find her keys. "Ugh. Why, why? Where did I put them?"

"What are you looking for and why do you look so frantic?" Jemma asked.

"I can't find my keys and I don't want to be late. I'm meeting Natasha for coffee."

"Oh, well, that's not like you."

Isabella looked up from where she was checking the seat cushions. "Not helpful. Can you help me, please?"

Isabella hated how nervous she was feeling. Her stomach had been in knots ever since she'd made the appointment with Natasha earlier in the week. She also hadn't seen Thomas again since the day that they'd arrived—nearly a week ago. They had been texting but each time that she'd suggested they get together, Thomas seemed to have plans that he couldn't break. It was really starting to annoy her, or more honestly, hurt her feelings. She'd decided to let it go until after she had her coffee date with Natasha. Maybe that would shed some light on things. Maybe they'd end up becoming good friends and all would be good.

"Bella?"

"Huh? Did you find them?" Isabella looked over at Jemma, who was standing in the kitchen.

"Yep, right here on the counter where you always put them." Jemma laughed and tossed the keys to her.

Isabella sat down on the couch with a sigh. "Good grief. Thanks."

Jemma came into the living room and handed Isabella a cup of coffee. "Here. You need to drink this." She laughed. "Get a little caffeine in ya, pre-coffee date." She sat down in a chair opposite Isabella with her own cup of coffee. "Relax. I'm sure everything's going to be fine."

"Why do you think that? Thomas is acting so weird. I can't believe we've not seen him again since we arrived."

"Well, maybe he's just been busy."

"Doing what?"

Isabella knew she had a good counterpoint. Thomas was pretty much in vacation mode as far as she knew. It was unlikely that he didn't actually have time to spend with her, and in the back of her mind she knew that Natasha had something to do with it.

"Oh, I dunno, Bella. But why are you thinking the worst? Natasha seemed to like you just fine when we met her. I mean, she was a bit snooty in my opinion, but nothing big happened, right?"

"Right. Not really. Oh, I don't know. Maybe I'll get a clue today, I guess."

"Yeah. Maybe she just wants a chance to get to know you. I'm sure Thomas has talked a lot about you to her, so there could be a hint of jealousy there."

"Really? Natasha didn't strike me as the jealous type. She seemed so confident and sure of herself. And she's so much older than us. I'm the one who should be jealous of her. She really seems to have her act together."

"Yeah, but that's all surface stuff, right? She might be solid with her career but floundering in the love department."

"Ugh. I really hope we're not going to get too personal—when it comes to her and Thomas, I mean. That would just be weird."

"Well, time will tell, and on that note, you better get going, right?"

Isabella looked over at the clock. "Yes, I gotta run. Are you going to be around later?"

"For a debriefing? Are you kidding? I will await your return and take you to lunch as a reward for surviving."

Isabella laughed. "That's a plan. Okay, I'm off. Wish me luck."

"Just be yourself. She'll adore you just as everyone else does."

Jemma gave her a big hug and Isabella walked out the door to make her way to the tube station.

Isabella smoothed her skirt down and then glanced in

the window of the large building before entering. Thomas had texted her that the place Natasha was taking her was quite fancy—code for don't show up in your jeans. Now she wished that she'd have taken a bit more time with her hair and put on a little more make-up. She rode the elevator up to the top-floor cafe, feeling out of place the moment she stepped off.

She scanned the room as the hostess came over to her, and gestured to where Natasha sat at a table by the window. "I see my friend is here."

"Follow me, please."

Natasha glanced up from her phone just as Isabella came up to the table. She stood up to kiss her on each cheek.

"Isabella, thanks for meeting me. You look lovely."

So prim and proper. That was what felt stuffy to Isabella.

"Thanks for inviting me. And you look great too."

Natasha was wearing her suit; Isabella knew that she was meeting her during a work break. She willed herself to calm down. It was just a coffee, and everything was going to be fine. She sat down across from her and looked out the window.

"Wow. You weren't kidding about the view. This is fantastic."

"Yes, it is quite nice. I bring clients here often for meetings."

The waiter came over to take their espresso orders,

and Isabella could feel Natasha studying her intently. *Just be yourself, Isabella.*

"So, how are you and Jemma enjoying the city so far? Have you had a chance to see a lot?"

"Yes. We've done the tourist things—rode the double-decker bus and all that. There's still a lot we've not seen but Jemma's been here before and I've been pretty busy with some work."

"Oh yes. Thomas tells me that you're working on your first novel?"

"Yes, that's right."

Isabella really didn't want to talk about her book. She'd not even shared that much with Thomas, so she wasn't prepared to talk about it in any detail with Natasha.

"Who's your publisher?" Natasha asked.

Isabella felt her face grow warm. She hated this question. With some people there seemed to be such a stigma when it came to self-publishing. She had the sneaky suspicion that Natasha might be one of those types of people.

"Oh, I've decided to self-publish. I didn't even try to get an agent or anything. My book is really more of a personal goal, so it's not like I have huge expectations for it."

"Oh. I see. Well, I hope that it will do very well for you."

"Thank you." Isabella was happy for the distraction

of their waiter back with the coffees. "And what about you? Thomas told me that you are in the financial industry. Do you enjoy your job?"

Natasha put her coffee down and wiped her mouth with the cloth napkin from the table. "Yes. Yes, I do very much. It's more than a job to me, though. It's a career that I've been building over the past ten years. I'm sure that Thomas has told you that."

No, Thomas really hadn't told Isabella much of anything about Natasha's career aspirations. Thomas hadn't told Isabella much of anything at all about his girlfriend.

Isabella nodded in response, trying to think of a new topic of conversation. Before she could think of what to say, Natasha was speaking again, her demeanor very serious all of the sudden.

"Isabella, there's a reason why I wanted to speak with you."

"Okay."

"I know you are Thomas's best friend—which quite honestly I do find a bit odd—but that's besides the point."

"Why do you think that's odd?" Isabella was genuinely curious.

"Well, I mean it's not normal that your best friend is of the opposite sex. Quite frankly I have a hard time believing that you and Thomas have never been more than just friends. It's just not something that sits well with me."

Isabella felt her heartbeat quicken as a dozen responses entered her mind, one of which was to throw her glass of water across the table onto Natasha's perfectly groomed hair. Instead she took in a deep breath before she responded.

"Well, you're wrong about that, Natasha. There's never been anything between Thomas and me other than friendship. I'm sure he's told you that."

"He has. Yes." She looked at her from across the table and Isabella felt distinctly uncomfortable at the direction their conversation was going.

"Okay, so what did you want to speak to me about then?" Isabella was proud of the fact that her voice didn't waver. She could hold her own with Miss Fancy-Pants.

Isabella swore that she saw Natasha flinch slightly. She hadn't been expecting Isabella to speak her mind. She could tell that from the way the woman seemed a little less sure of herself.

"Well, I just wanted you to know that I'm very serious about Thomas—about our relationship. To be quite frank with you, I want to be married and having kids within the year."

Isabella nearly choked on the sip of coffee she'd just taken.

"Oh, I'm not telling you anything that Thomas doesn't know. He's well aware and completely on board."

"Really?"

"Why are you so surprised by that?"

"Well, Thomas is my best friend of ten years. I know him pretty well. I find it hard to believe that he's ready to settle down at this stage in his life. Obviously he's a lot younger than you and I'm not sure it's fair to be putting that kind of pressure on him."

"I'm not pressuring him, Isabella. Thomas loves me."

Isabella felt sick to her stomach. She really didn't know quite how to respond to this conversation, and all she wanted to do was run out of the building. She wasn't liking Natasha any better at all.

"Natasha, why are you telling me this?" Isabella looked at her intently. She could be straightforward too.

Natasha looked slightly taken aback. "I just wanted you to know in the hopes that you might back off a bit with Thomas."

"Back off? I'm not sure what you're getting at. I haven't even seen Thomas since we arrived. And furthermore, I actually think you have a lot of nerve saying such a thing to me. He and I have been there for one another for the past ten years, and I'm not about to promise you anything when it comes to my relationship with him. I'm pretty sure that Thomas can tell me himself if he thinks things need to change in our relationship."

"Oh? So why do you think he's not seen you since you arrived here?"

The look on Natasha's face was smug, and it was all Isabella could do to keep from slapping her across the face. She refrained, getting up quickly from her chair.

"Look, Natasha. I don't know why you seem to have such a problem with me. I was really hoping that you and I would be friends. I think it would be in your best interest and mine, since we both care about Thomas so much. I'm not going to sit here and listen to you insult me or try to tell me how Thomas feels. Thomas can tell me himself, which I'm sure he will do. Thanks for the coffee and have a lovely day."

With that, Isabella turned away, walking quickly out of the restaurant and onto the elevator. She was desperate to get some air and calm her anger, which had surprised her. Apparently she could be quite defensive when it came to her relationship with Thomas.

The moment she stepped outside and walked around to the side of the building, she burst into tears. This was a nightmare. Natasha was a nightmare. How could Thomas possibly be in love with that woman? She wouldn't believe it. It was time for him to be straight with her.

Isabella grabbed her phone out of her purse and punched in a text to him.

Thomas, we need to talk. When can you meet me?

She waited. He'd get back to her. At least he had been replying to her texts. Unless, of course, he was hearing otherwise from Natasha right this minute. She couldn't escape the ugly thought that Natasha would be so bold. Her phone dinged with the incoming response.

Are you okay? Coffee didn't go well, I take it?

No, it did not. And I want to talk to YOU about things. Lunch tomorrow? Please?

She waited another few seconds for his response. She rolled her eyes. Checking his busy calendar. Yeah, right. More likely it seemed that he might be checking with Natasha.

OK. I'll come pick you up at 1 tomorrow.

Perfect. See you then.

She'd get to the bottom of this nonsense and hopefully knock some sense into her best friend's apparently lovesick brain.

CHAPTER 13

Isabella sat at the kitchen table across from Jemma, fuming still from the words Natasha had said to her.

"I mean seriously? How dare she think that she can just declare my friendship with Thomas to be over? She's got some nerve, and why she thinks that would ever fly with Thomas is beyond me—"

"—Bella, slow down. Good grief, girl. Tell me what happened. I don't think I've ever seen you this angry before."

Isabella took a deep breath to keep from crying. She was angry—very angry—but deep down she was also afraid. Could Natasha actually take Thomas from her? The thought sickened her. More so that he'd ever let that happen, but he'd been acting so weird lately that she was more than a little confused about their relationship.

She finally sat still for a few minutes and Jemma waited without saying anything, most likely waiting for Isabella to gather her wits about her enough to speak about what had happened. She filled Jemma in on the entire conversation and waited for her response. Jemma would help her to know what to do—how to handle things. She'd become a good voice of reason to Isabella over their past months together.

"Wow. I don't know why I'm so surprised, but I guess I am. Who does she think she is anyway? Don't you think she would wonder how all this was going to fly with Thomas? I wonder if he even knew what she was going to talk to you about."

"Well, I know. That was my thought too. I did text him—right afterwards, actually."

"And? Did you talk to him?"

"No, we're having lunch together tomorrow."

"Well, that's good."

Isabella couldn't keep her emotions in any longer, as hard as she was trying to.

"Hey, don't cry." Jemma came over to the other side of the table to lean down and hug Isabella. "I'm sure everything's going to be fine—that it's just some massive misunderstanding."

Isabella wiped at her eyes with her hand. "Do you think it's true? What Natasha said about Thomas being in love with her?"

"I don't know. It could be. But do I think that's gonna make him stop being friends with you? Not a chance." Jemma sat down in the chair next to Isabella, watching her quietly for a few moments before she spoke again. "Bella?"

"Yeah?"

"Be honest with me."

Isabella nodded her head.

"Are you more upset about the possibility of your friendship with Thomas changing or the fact that Natasha told you that he loved her?"

"I think it's that I'm afraid she's going to take him away from me—that everything about the friendship that we've had for so long is going to change. I don't want that to happen."

"Okay. I understand you being upset about that, but to play devil's advocate for a minute—if they are in love—heck, let's say they even get engaged…"

Isabella looked up quickly at Jemma's words. "Jem, don't say that." Even the thought of Thomas being engaged to that woman made her feel sick to her stomach.

"Well, I'm just saying—let's suppose that it happened. If it were me, I'd be a little leery of my future husband having a best friend that was a woman—especially after seeing the two of you together. You gotta realize that at least somewhat, Bella."

Isabella sighed. She knew that Jemma had a point. Relationships changed over time, and it wasn't realistic to think that she and Thomas would have the same level of closeness once either of them were married or to the point of being that serious about their significant other. She did get that.

"I guess you do have a good point. I need to prepare myself and probably realize that Thomas and I shouldn't be as close as we are."

"Well, I don't know about that, but you know I have my opinions about the two of you." Jemma smiled. "You can only go on what he tells you, I guess. Hopefully he's going to be honest with you tomorrow and then you can just go from there. Oh, and for the record, I hope he doesn't end up with Natasha. Personally, I don't think they are right for one another at all."

Isabella laughed. "Thank you for saying that."

CHAPTER 14

Thomas was holding the door to the pub open for her, waiting for her to close her umbrella and get in out of the rain. He put his hand lightly on her back and led her inside.

"What's up with this rain, huh?" Isabella asked— knowing that a conversation about the weather was all she could handle until they were sitting down across from one another, where she could look him in the eyes.

"No kidding. I guess it's time to get my winter sweaters out." Thomas laughed. "You're looking pretty cozy in yours, I must say. I love that color blue on you."

Isabella smiled and then just as quickly felt that moment of panic in her gut. This was what she would miss. Thomas had always been the one to lift her spirits— to say the kindest things to her whenever she'd been feeling down. She just couldn't imagine that going away. She'd do whatever she could to prevent that from happening.

Instead of saying any of that just yet, she smiled

across the table at him. "Thank you. You're always so sweet to me."

The waiter came over to take their orders, and they continued to make small talk until their food came.

Finally, Isabella couldn't stand it any longer. She had to just get it out. Not talking about what was really bothering her wasn't going to make things go away, and she was a little miffed that Thomas was apparently waiting for her to bring up the subject of Natasha.

"So, does Natasha know that we're having lunch today?"

"She does. Yes."

Isabella thought he was already looking uncomfortable, but she was prepared to go ahead with the conversation that she'd rehearsed in her head over and over that morning.

"So, did she tell you about our coffee meeting— everything that was said? And pretty much how horrible she was to me?"

She noticed his jaw clench as she waited for his response.

"Well, she told me that you stormed out of the restaurant. She kinda made it sound like you didn't really give her a chance to finish the conversation. Maybe if you'd stayed to talk, the whole thing wouldn't have gone so wrong." Thomas ran his hand through his hair, something Isabella knew that he did whenever he was nervous.

"Thomas. Seriously?"

"Iz, what do you expect me to do? I feel like I'm totally caught in the middle here."

"I don't know, Thomas, but what I don't expect is that you'd just throw away our years of friendship over a woman you barely know." As much as she was trying not to cry, she could feel tears burning behind her eyelids.

"Iz, come on. Stop being so dramatic. Who said anything about me throwing away our friendship? Do you really think I'd do that?"

She couldn't contain her tears, much as she was trying to hold them back. She put her fingertips to her forehead, her hands shielding her eyes as her tears fell freely.

She felt Thomas come around the booth to sit next to her, his hand immediately rubbing her back.

"Iz, don't cry. Come on. Please stop."

She felt his breath on her ear as he gave her a quick kiss there and pulled her in tight against his chest. She let her head relax, her sobs slowing and finally her arms going around the boy—who wasn't a boy at all any more—whose comfort she knew so well. Being in Thomas's arms felt natural to her. It had always been the one place she could count on when anything bad had been going on in her life. She felt his hand rubbing her back again and his kiss on her forehead.

Isabella started to giggle.

"Hey, what's so funny?" Thomas pushed her up away from him gently, so that he could look her in the face.

"Do you think maybe this is why Natasha has a problem with me? I mean look at us, Thomas." Isabella was still giggling. "Is this how most friends behave together?"

Thomas was shaking his head, grinning as he handed Isabella a napkin. "Here, wipe your face, goofball."

He was still looking at her intently as she finally stopped giggling and blowing her nose loudly. She moved over on the seat a bit to create a little space between them, aware that Thomas was still watching her with a strange look on his face.

"So, are you okay now? With your breakdown, I mean?" He winked at her and she nodded in response as he moved back to the other side of the table, still watching her, all signs of the earlier discomfort between them gone.

Isabella took a sip of her drink and tried to think about what else needed to be discussed. She felt emotionally drained and didn't know if she had it in her to finish the conversation that they probably did still need to have.

"In answer to your question—"

Isabella looked over at him, feeling confused as to what he was referring to.

"—about how we behave together…"

Isabella felt her face go warm. She'd used the words herself, but hearing Thomas say them made her heart pound faster.

"Yeah, what about it?" She forced the question out.

"Iz, the truth is, I don't know another way to behave with you. You're so incredibly important to me. I care about your feelings and I never want to hurt you—to make you cry. You have to know that. I can't imagine not having you in my life. It's not what I want at all, okay?"

"Okay, but what about Natasha? Everything she said to me? Thomas, you do know that what *she* really wants is to be married and start having kids."

She could see the tension in Thomas's jaw again.

"Yeah, Iz. I suppose I do know that. I mean, we've talked about it."

"You have?" Isabella felt sick to her stomach again. She wanted everything that Natasha had said to her to be lies or some kind of miscommunication between herself and Thomas.

"Well, yeah. I mean, I have to respect where she is in her life. Wanting kids and all? I kinda knew that when we first got involved, I suppose."

"So that's what you want? I'm sorry. I just find that so hard to believe."

Thomas was looking at her with an odd smile on his face.

"Why? Why is it so hard to imagine that I'd want to settle down—to have a family? I do want those things."

"Right. That's not hard for me to imagine at all. I think you'll be a great father one day—the key phrase being *one day*. I guess I just figured that you still had some wild oats to sow or something." Isabella laughed, trying to lighten the mood. "I don't know. I suppose its none of my business, but the more bothersome part of what Natasha and I talked about yesterday was the fact that it seems she doesn't want us to spend any time together."

Thomas was nodding his head. "Yes, honestly, Iz— between you and me—that bothers me too. A lot. I would say that it's the single biggest argument Natasha and I have been having lately. I can't get her to understand how important your friendship is to me. And believe me, I've been trying."

Nothing was exactly right, but somehow hearing the words Thomas was saying was making Isabella feel better and a bit more secure with their friendship.

"So, I'm guessing that this means you're definitely not coming to Ireland with Jemma and me?"

Thomas sighed. "I really wanted to. We've been planning this trip for so long and somehow I know that I've managed to ruin all of that—at least in terms of you and me traveling together. But I think I have to stick this out—see what happens between Natasha and me. If I go to Ireland, I honestly think it would be over between us, and I'm just not ready to do that. I know it seems kinda crazy and I can't explain it, but I feel a sense of commitment with her that I've not really felt before."

Isabella hated hearing the words but she couldn't fault him. He looked so vulnerable pouring out the truth about how he was feeling.

She reached over to take his hand across the table. "It's okay. I do understand—or I will understand. I feel better now after we've talked, less likely that you're just kicking me to the curb." She laughed.

"No, Iz. I'm definitely not kicking you to the curb. I'm just asking you for a little patience. I think if I can just focus on Natasha and our relationship for a while—until she feels a little more secure—then I think she'll come around. I'm putting my money on you two becoming friends in the near future."

Isabella laughed. "Well, I'm not sure that I'd be holding my breath on that one."

"We'll see. Now can we please talk about something else? You still haven't told me about your father and the San Francisco trip you have planned, and I'm dying to know everything."

Isabella filled Thomas in on all the details that she'd not yet told him, happy for their familiar banter, yet at the same time dreading the meal coming to an end. She felt instinctively that it would be a long while before she saw her best friend again—before she had him to herself again, if she ever would.

CHAPTER 15

Isabella laughed as she settled in next to Jemma on the plane.

"What's so funny? You weren't laughing a few hours ago when we thought we were going to miss our flight."

"Sorry. I know. I'm terrible for leaving all that stuff to the last minute, but you know what?"

"What?" Jemma smiled at her.

"I'm done. Completely finished, and I am so ready for a proper vacation. Jemma, please tell me that we're going to have a blast this trip?"

Their last few weeks in London had flown by. Ever since Isabella had last seen Thomas—ever since they'd had their big talk—she'd really tried to give him and their relationship some space. And it *had* worked in terms of helping her to feel better about things. She needed to let Thomas do whatever he needed to do with Natasha, and she needed to be in a place where she could see her life without his playing such a big role in it.

So she'd spent her remaining days in London pouring herself into her book. She'd completed the final edits and sent it off to the person who was doing all the formatting for her. She'd been assured that the electronic version of her book would be hitting the virtual shelves any day now, and she'd be receiving the physical copies that she had on order well before Christmas.

"Hello? Earth to Miss Party Girl..."

"Oh, sorry. I totally spaced out there. You were saying?"

"I was just saying how proud of you I am and how much you deserve this trip. And I'm pleased at the way you've handled everything between you and Thomas. I'm sorry that the trip changed—that you're stuck with just me—but I'm glad to hear that you're as excited about it as I am."

"Jem, don't be silly. I hope you don't really feel that way. I'd be more disappointed if you'd have told me that you weren't going on the trip. You're my travel partner and don't you forget it."

"Well, for once, I kinda feel like we're in the same place with this one—both wanting to relax and see a bit of the country—"

"—Maybe meet some cute guys..."

Jemma looked at her with a funny expression of shock on her face. "Who are you and what have you done with my best friend?"

Isabella laughed. "Hey, it's about time I let my hair down a little bit. I've been hard at work on the book and a little stressed out about other things—but now? Now I just want to have a good time, with no worries about anything or anyone else. And I do hope there will be dancing."

Jemma grinned. "Oh, there will be dancing alright. I've already researched a couple of clubs we can get into in Dublin. Oh, yeah. My party girl Bella is back."

Isabella smiled and laid her head back against the seat. She was back, alright. It felt good to not be worried or consumed by anything. Thomas had called her the night before to wish her a good trip. The call had been brief, and Natasha was there in the background giving her regards via Thomas. And it hadn't really felt too awkward. Isabella had told herself that it was the new normal that she'd have to get used to—that she would just have to be content to follow Thomas's lead on what was going to happen with their friendship.

In her mind she was moving on from it all, determined to put herself in a space where she was open to meeting new people and new relationships. If that happened to include a new man in her life, she'd be open to that as well—starting with this trip to Ireland.

PAULA KAY

CHAPTER 16

Isabella laughed as Jemma grabbed her hand to drag her back onto the dance floor. "Jem, hold on. Let me grab my Coke."

Jemma nodded her head. "Hurry."

They'd been very careful throughout their travels whenever they'd been out. Their rules were simple. No alcohol, no leaving your drink behind where someone could put something in it, and no leaving a club without the other one. They were good girls anyway—not ones to really party hard—but they loved to have a good time dancing the night away.

Jemma had had some crazier days when she was younger, but she'd told Isabella early on that those days were far behind her. Now, mainly they just liked to have a laugh and enjoy the music in a good club.

This was the second night in a row that they'd been out dancing since arriving in Dublin a week earlier, and it was shaping up to be another night to add to Isabella's scrapbook of great memories together. She pulled her phone out to snap a selfie of them together on the dance floor.

"Bella, that guy over there is really checking you out."

"Huh? What guy?"

"Two o'clock—dark hair, black shirt."

Isabella looked to where Jemma was staring and then quickly looked away when the guy looked directly at her.

"Oh, wow. That's embarrassing. How is it that I don't know how to behave like a normal person in a club? And he's cute, right?"

"Very. At least smile at him." Jemma laughed and then tugged at Isabella's hand again. "Come on. Let's go back to our table and see if he comes over. But when we walk past him, give him a smile—a big gorgeous one!"

"Yes, ma'am." Isabella laughed, and when they walked past where Mister Hottie was sitting, she did make quick eye contact with him, giving him a wide grin. "Wow! I really need to get out more. My heart is racing."

"Well, don't look now, but here he comes." Jemma grinned.

Isabella adjusted her hair and picked up her glass to take a drink, willing herself to be natural and not as nervous as she felt.

"Hi. How are you girls doing tonight?" He directed the question toward both of them but there was no mistaking it when his eyes found their way back to Isabella.

"Hi, we're great, thanks. How are you?"

"Very good, thanks. I'm Colin." He stuck his hand

out toward Isabella and she grasped it firmly. "And you are?"

"Isabella, and this is Jemma."

He shook Jemma's hand also and then gestured toward the seat next to Isabella. "Do you mind if I sit down?"

"No. No, not all."

"So—Isabella. What a beautiful name."

She smiled at him. "My friends call my Bella—or Izzy—but mostly Bella these days."

"Well, I love all those names. Can I choose then?" He pulled out his phone. "Which name I'd like to put in my phone with your number?"

Isabella laughed. "Smooth."

"You think so?" He laughed also.

"Why don't we wait on that? I don't typically give my number out to strange guys that I meet in a club."

Isabella noticed Jemma grinning at her. She was doing an excellent job with her flirting practice, if she did say so herself. She was enjoying the attention that the handsome guy was giving her and the whole thing seemed amusing to Jemma, who had excused herself to find the ladies' room.

"So, Isabella. Would you dance with me?"

There was a slower song playing—a ballad that Isabella actually really loved.

She nodded her head and stood up from her chair, enjoying the feel of the stranger's hand in her own as he led her out to the dance floor. She caught Jemma's eye as she returned to their table and laughed lightly when she gave her a thumbs up.

"What's so funny, lovely Isabella?"

"Oh, nothing. And I do like how you say my name."

He leaned his head back so that he was studying her face. "Do you now?"

"Yes, I like the accent. I take it you're from here?"

"Ireland, yes. But not Dublin. I'm here with a couple of buddies for a stag party."

"Stag party? What's that?"

"Oh, I think you Americans call it a bachelor party. It's for a good friend of mine, and we're leaving the day after tomorrow to go home."

"So, where's home then?"

"I was hoping you'd ask." Colin winked at her.

Isabella liked the way he teased her. "Go on then. Don't keep me waiting." She grinned, enjoying their flirtation and the way she felt him pull her just a little bit closer when he laughed at her comment.

"Oh don't you worry. I'd never keep a girl like you waiting."

"A girl like me? But you don't know anything about me."

"I know that you're the most gorgeous creature I've ever laid eyes on."

"Stop. Now you're really laying it on thick."

"I'm not. Surely you must know how beautiful you

are."

"You were saying—about where you live?"

"If I tell you, will you promise to come visit?"

"I can't make promises like that. I'm with my friend. But you already know that."

"Well, I can promise you that you won't be disappointed."

"Oh, really now. That's a very bold statement."

He laughed and Isabella thought how much she liked the sound of his voice. It was impossible not to smile when he spoke.

"You've heard of the Ring of Kerry, have you?"

"The part of Ireland where a lot of the postcard pictures are from?"

"Yes, that's right. County Kerry is one of the most visited parts of Ireland, and I live in a place called Killarney, which is also quite popular with tourists. I'm not exaggerating when I tell you how beautiful it is there and when you come, I promise to show you—and your friend Jemma, of course—a really nice time."

"Is that so?"

"It is. It is so, my lady."

Isabella laughed and then glanced over to where Jemma sat at their table.

"Colin, it's been really nice meeting you, but I'm afraid I should get going. I don't want to leave Jemma sitting there alone for longer."

"Sure. But you can't possibly think I'm really going to

let you go without getting your phone number. We have so much to talk about yet. I want to find out everything there is to know about you."

He was grinning at her, and Isabella bit her bottom lip as she thought about what to do. It couldn't hurt—giving him her number. And she and Jemma really didn't know if they were going to travel beyond Dublin. They hadn't gotten that far in their planning, and in case they did make it to this Killarney place, it might be good to have a contact there.

She laughed lightly as she realized that she was trying to find so many good reasons for giving this nice enough guy her phone number, when the plain truth of the matter was that she was attracted to him. He was making her feel better than she'd felt in a long time—and what was the harm in talking to him further? Besides, chances were he wouldn't call her anyway.

She stuck out her hand.

"Yes?"

"Your phone, kind sir?" She smiled as he grinned back at her, slipping the phone in her palm.

"Let's put it under Isabella then, shall we?"

"We shall." Isabella put her number in and handed him back the phone, not missing the amused look that Jemma was sending her way. She stuck out her hand. "So, it was very nice meeting you, Colin. Thank you for the dance."

He held her hand, but then gestured to his cheek.

"How bout one little kiss? For good luck."

Isabella laughed and kissed his cheek quickly, but not quick enough that she didn't notice how nice he smelled.

"Thank you very much." He turned toward Jemma. "Jemma, it was nice meeting you. Enjoy your stay in Ireland." Then he pulled Isabella in for a hug. "Isabella, I will be calling you soon and if I might be so lucky, I hope to see you soon as well."

With that he was off, and Isabella and Jemma sat at the small table staring at one another.

"Well done, little Miss I-don't-know-how-to-flirt-at-all." Jemma was laughing.

"Well, he was cute, wasn't he?"

"Oh, he was cute alright. You're going to have to tell me what that was all about and when you might be seeing him next."

"I'll tell you all about it. Are you ready to go?"

Jemma nodded and they headed outside to hail a taxi, Isabella feeling quite satisfied with how the night had gone. Meeting Colin had been a good distraction for her, even if nothing else came of it.

PAULA KAY

CHAPTER 17

Isabella clicked off the video chat with Lucas, just as Jemma came into the kitchen.

"Oh, sorry, Jem. I hope I didn't wake you. The Wi-Fi is so much better out here, and I really needed to connect with Lucas about Thanksgiving."

"No, I was awake. How's everything with your father? I bet they're getting anxious to see you."

"My father. That seems weird, calling him that. I mean, I have a dad, right?"

"Yes, you do. And now you have two, I guess." Jemma grinned. "So? Are all the plans made? I still feel so bad that you're going alone."

"I know. It's okay. I know you'd go with me if you could. I am nervous, or at least I will be. Right now I'm pretty excited about it, though."

"I'll bet. It's a special thing for both of you. And your parents? How are they handling everything?"

"Wow. My parents have just been so incredibly supportive. I still can't get over it. It really just seems like my whole family keeps getting bigger and everyone is so welcoming with them also. It feels really good, you know?"

"I'll bet."

Isabella's phone rang where she'd set it on the table. She reached over to check the number, setting it back down when she didn't recognize it.

"You're not going to answer it?" Jemma asked.

Isabella shrugged. "Probably a wrong number."

"Or it could be Colin." Jemma grinned and grabbed Isabella's phone up off the table.

"Hello? Oh, hey, Colin. No, this is Jemma. Hold on, Bella's right here."

Jemma handed her the phone and Isabella felt her mouth go dry. She really couldn't believe that he was calling her so soon—or calling her at all for that matter.

"Hello?"

"Hey, beautiful. Remember me?"

Isabella laughed the moment she heard his voice and silly joke. "Of course I remember you. You're not easy to forget."

Jemma rolled her eyes across the table from her and gave her a thumbs-up.

"Well, in that case, you should instantly say yes to my invitation for today. I promise you a good time. I promise you a wonderful tour of the city aboard one of those cool buses where we can sit on the second level, enjoying the slightly rainy weather while we sip coffees and hold hands under a blanket."

Isabella laughed. "You're pretty sure of yourself, aren't you?"

"I'm sure that we'll have a good time together, if that's what you mean."

"So what time are you thinking for this little tour?"

"In an hour? Oh, and invite Jemma along also."

"Can I phone you back? I have your number now."

"Do you promise you will?"

Isabella laughed. "Yes. I'll phone you back in five minutes. And Colin?"

"Yes, my darling."

Isabella felt a slight pull in her gut. The way he'd spoken reminded her of the way that Thomas so often teased her. But she wasn't thinking about Thomas on this trip. She was moving on herself—with new people and new adventures of her own.

"Hello? You were saying?"

Colin's voice in her ear reminded her that she was still on the phone with him.

"Oh, sorry. I was just going to say thanks for calling."

"Of course. Phone me back in five."

Isabella hung up and grinned at Jemma, who'd just gotten back to the table with a cup of coffee.

"So do tell? What was that all about?"

"It was an invitation."

Jemma raised an eyebrow. "Go on."

"For both of us, by the way..."

"Mm-hm."

"He wants to know if we would like to do a city tour. On one of those two-level buses." Isabella looked at the time on her phone. "In about an hour."

"Go—get ready!"

"Are you coming?"

"Nope. I'm not going to be a third wheel on this date of yours." Jemma laughed. "Seriously. It's okay. I have things I want to get done here. And I'm excited for you, Bella. It's nice to see you going out on a date."

Isabella grinned. "It has been a long time."

"Yes, it has. Now call him back and go get ready. Wear something cute."

"Does that mean I can raid your closet?"

"You may. Go!"

Isabella stole a glance at Colin sitting next to her on top of the bus. True to his word, he'd met her at the tour bus stop right on time with coffees and a blanket. They'd been riding now for about fifteen minutes and Isabella was intensely aware of her hand inside his under the blanket. It felt good—being romanced by a guy, especially one as cute as Colin.

They'd been chatting nonstop since they'd boarded the bus. Isabella had filled him in on some of the details of her life—where she was from, what she and Jemma had been doing on their travels—but nothing of much importance. There'd be time for that later, if they'd be keeping in touch at all.

Colin squeezed her hand and she felt the intensity of his stare.

"You're really beautiful, Isabella. I don't want to stop looking at you. Maybe you should come home with me today."

"Colin! Don't be silly." Isabella felt herself blushing. It was a lot of attention to have all at once. "I haven't talked to Jemma yet about our travel plans, but we won't be leaving Dublin before the end of the week."

"And then? How much time will you spend in Ireland and what will you do after that?"

Isabella caught herself before blurting out her plans. She didn't want to get into all the details about her family life—about meeting her birth father in just a few weeks. That all seemed a bit too intense for first-date conversation.

"We have to be back in London in two weeks or so. I have a flight to San Francisco—to spend Thanksgiving with my family."

"Okay, good. So that means you might want to take about a week or so to come down south to see me—I mean, to see the Ring of Kerry—one of the most beautiful spots in Ireland, not to be missed, I might add."

Isabella laughed. "So you've said."

Colin leaned over to kiss her cheek. "I have to see you again, Isabella."

Isabella's heart beat faster and when she turned just a

PAULA KAY

bit to look at him, his hand came to the side of her face, drawing her to him for a deep kiss. It was unexpected and nice.

"Wow. I could kiss you for days. Yeah. I'm gonna want to do that some more."

Isabella smiled widely. "That was pretty nice."

"Shall we do it again?" He grinned like a little boy and didn't wait for her answer as he pulled her to him under the blanket, kissing her again until she had to pull away a bit to get a breath.

When she felt his hand on her thigh, she put her own on top of it. "Let's not get carried away now. We are in public."

It wasn't the only reason she didn't want things to move too fast though. Isabella didn't have a lot of experience with men. Maybe she was looking for a distraction, but she wasn't looking to get into anything too fast. She knew better than that—how that sort of thing could derail one's plans.

Just as she was having the thought, the words of Arianna's letter to her came to mind. Finding love—was that what she was doing? At some point in her life, she did have to start taking more chances—with relationships, with men. She looked over at Colin, who was watching something that the bus driver had been pointing out. But was Colin the one? In her hearts of hearts, she doubted it, but her doubts had led her down the wrong path in the past.

He looked over at her, leaning in for another quick kiss, which Isabella happily gave him. Right now she was feeling content—happy to be wanted by a man—and for now she'd just let that feeling be enough, not thinking about more than that.

PAULA KAY

CHAPTER 18

Isabella looked toward Jemma in the backseat of the convertible that Colin was driving. She was laughing at something that Colin's friend, Sean, was saying and Isabella thought that the two of them seemed to be hitting it off quite nicely.

Finally, after much debate, she and Jemma had decided a few days ago that the Ring of Kerry really was a not-to-be-missed sight for them while they were in Ireland. Isabella had been talking to Colin daily since he'd left Dublin, and he was more than happy to get them set up in a nice little bed and breakfast in Killarney.

Colin had wanted Isabella to stay with him, but she didn't lose time shooting down that idea. She was a long way from spending the night with him, if it ever came to that. She wanted to see him, but she also wanted to spend time with Jemma, just as they'd always done while on their travels.

Today, he'd hired a convertible and come to take them for the famous drive along the Ring of Kerry. He'd packed a picnic and brought along a good friend who he'd told Isabella would be perfect for Jemma.

As Colin pulled the car off to the side of the road, Isabella looked out over the banks to the wide sea stretched beyond. It was a gorgeous day—something that Colin had said was a small miracle around there—and Isabella was feeling very content and lucky to be there.

"Who's ready for some food?" Colin asked.

Isabella and Jemma looked at one another.

"I'm starving actually," said Jemma.

"Me too. What you do have?" Isabella grinned as she walked around to get the large picnic basket.

Colin kissed her on the cheek, taking the basket from her. "Let me get that, my love. If you could just grab that blanket from the back, that would be perfect."

Jemma came over to whisper in Isabella's ear as the guys started walking to find a good spot for their picnic. "My love?"

Isabella laughed, whispering back. "It's just a term of endearment they use here, silly."

"Oh, I know, and I think he's quite smitten with you." Jemma smiled. "Do you like him? That much, I mean?"

Isabella shrugged. "He makes me feel good, I guess. When I'm around him. I do like him. Oh, I don't know. It's too soon to tell, isn't it?" She reached down to get the blanket from the backseat of the car.

"Are you girls coming, or what?" Colin called over to them.

"Yep. Right now." Isabella linked arms with Jemma. "We'll talk about it more later but tell me—what do you think of Sean?"

It was Jemma's turn to shrug. "He's nice—pretty funny."

"But no potential love match, I take it?"

"Nope. But that's okay. I'm happy to be chaperoning this date with you and your man." Jemma winked at her and the two headed to where the guys were waiting.

"Colin, that was really fantastic," Jemma said as she leaned back on her elbows. "Thanks for organizing all that food. I'm ready for a nap now." She curled up slightly on the blanket in the space left empty by Sean, who'd gone off to make a phone call.

Colin stood, reaching for Isabella's hand. "Who's up for a little walk? There's a path just down there a ways that leads to an even more spectacular view."

Isabella let him pull her to her feet. "That sounds like a good idea to me. Jem?"

"Nah, you two go on. I was serious about my little nap."

Isabella and Colin hadn't gotten too far when Jemma called out to Isabella with her phone in hand.

"It's Thomas." She mouthed the word "sorry" to her.

Isabella returned and looked down at her phone, realizing that Thomas was on video chat. *Thanks, Jemma.*

Although maybe Thomas seeing her with a guy wasn't such a bad thing. She couldn't help the thought.

She held the phone up so that her face filled Thomas's screen, noticing that Colin had a look of total confusion on his face. She'd probably have to fill him in just a bit, but she'd deal with that later.

"Hey, Thomas. Long time, no chat." She grinned into the phone.

"Hey, yourself. I've been missing you—wanting to see your beautiful face."

Isabella felt Colin behind her grabbing for her hand. She quickly switched the phone camera.

"Hey, check out where I am right now. It's so gorgeous. You'd love it here. We're at the Ring of Kerry." She moved the phone slowly as she rotated her body so that Thomas could see the view.

"Looks wonderful. I wish I were there with you guys. Give me back your face, Iz." Thomas laughed.

Colin squeezed her tightly to him and it was all she could do to keep from shoving him away. It was obvious that he wasn't going to give her any privacy right now. She took a breath and turned the camera direction so it was facing her now.

"Hey, Thomas, I want you to meet a friend of mine."

Colin stuck his hand out in a wave. "Hiya."

"Thomas, this is Colin. Colin, this is my friend Thomas—my best friend since we were kids." She squeezed Colin's hand as she introduced the two.

She thought she saw Thomas's expression change just a bit. They had been communicating a little since she and Jemma had left London, but she'd not told him anything about meeting Colin. Not that she was keeping it from him, she just wasn't sure that there was anything to tell yet.

"Great to meet you, Colin," Thomas was saying from the other end of the phone.

"You too, mate. Well, I'll leave you two be." He leaned in to kiss Isabella on the cheek. "Don't be long, hon. We still have a bit of a drive ahead of us."

Isabella nodded and then went over to sit on a rock.

"Hon?"

"Oh, it's nothing, Thomas."

"Hmm—maybe you should tell that to him. I saw the way he was looking at you."

"We'll talk about that later. How are you? Is everything good?"

Thomas's expression seemed to darken. "Yeah, you know. Everything's fine."

"Meaning? I don't want to pry into your business— you know that—but I have to ask. Are things okay with Natasha?"

"Things are okay, yes. She's got this big wedding coming up—her cousin, I think it is. So we've had a few parties and related festivities. It's apparently an even bigger event around here than any wedding I've ever seen."

"Interesting."

"What?"

"Well, I can't help but think that that could be you not long from now—preparing for a big to-do wedding."

"Iz, please don't start with that."

"I'm sorry. Okay. I miss you. I really do."

"I miss you too. Tell me about San Francisco. Is it next week already? How are you feeling, Iz? Are you nervous?"

"Yes, it's next week and yes, I'm starting to feel nervous about it. I hope I don't freak out. You know how I get."

"How you used to get, you mean?" Thomas grinned at her. "You've come a long way. I don't really think that you're the freak-out type—not any more. Remember that."

"Thanks." She felt a huge sense of relief even talking to him, but it made her wish he was there, traveling with them even despite the fact that she seemed to have Colin now.

"So, Jemma really can't go with you?"

"No, she's meeting her mom in London. It was planned a long time ago. She offered to cancel and come with me, but I didn't want her to change her plans. Yeah, it would be nice to have her going with me, but I'll be okay. I can handle it."

"I know you can. I'm pretty sure that you can handle anything."

"You think? That's quite a compliment coming from you."

"What, that I think you're pretty amazing?" Thomas grinned.

Isabella noticed Colin motioning for her near the car.

"Thomas, sorry. I gotta go. It was nice chatting. I'm happy you called."

"Me too, Iz. Have fun. Iz? Don't have too much fun—with Colin, I mean."

Was that jealousy she detected or just Thomas's normal teasing?

"It's pretty casual, Thomas. Nothing too serious."

"If you say so."

"I do. Now I gotta run. Miss you."

"Miss you more. Bye."

Isabella and Jemma spent their remaining week in Ireland touring a bit in the south and then making their way back to Dublin for a few nights before they were to fly out. Isabella had only spent the few days with Colin while they were in Killarney, even though he'd begged her to stay longer. She liked him, but she had to be honest with herself that there wasn't a future between them—not with her leaving and him back at his job and real life. They had promised to keep in touch though, and so far he'd been pretty persistent about calling her daily.

When the time came to fly back to London, Isabella

was ready for it. Not so much because she didn't care to spend more time touring Ireland, but more because her next adventure was looking to be her biggest one yet— meeting her father and sister. She was now officially feeling nervous about it, and it was all she could think about during their last days in Ireland.

CHAPTER 19

"Thanks for waiting around with me, Jem. You don't have to if you want to get going." Isabella glanced at her phone to see that she still had two hours before her flight was to leave London. "I'm sure your mom is very anxious to see you."

"Mom's at a meeting and we're getting together for lunch after, so I'm here to keep you company until—" Jemma looked down at her phone.

"Yes?"

"Huh?"

"Jem, why are you acting so weird and distracted? Expecting an important message from your new boyfriend that you've not told me about?" Isabella laughed.

"Oh—uh, sorry—just watching for a text from my mom."

"You were saying? You're going to wait with me until my flight boards?"

"Yep." Jemma grinned, then her face got more

131

serious. "So how are you feeling about everything?"

"Everything meaning Colin?"

"Well I was referring to the meeting with your father, but we can talk about boys if you'd rather. And while we're on the subject, what's going on with you and Thomas? Is everything alright now between you two?"

Isabella felt her mood shift at the mention of Thomas's name. It hurt her stomach to think about him and the weirdness with their relationship. It was so odd to her—feeling like they really didn't know what was going on in one another's lives. She hated it.

"No, not exactly. I don't know, Jemma. We talked a few times and things seem fine on the phone, but I just feel pretty bad about everything. I should have just minded my own business when it comes to his relationship. I'm the one that started all this mess, so it's probably up to me to fix it, I suppose."

"With Natasha, you mean? Hopefully she'll get over what was bothering her so much, now that she's had Thomas all to herself again." Jemma's phone dinged with a text.

"Your mom?"

"Mm-hm."

Jemma seemed distracted again as she sent off a reply. She smiled as she read the response that came straight back.

"Okay, so I really am starting to believe that you have a secret boyfriend now." Isabella laughed.

"I'm sorry. Mom's just being silly." Jemma tucked her phone back into her purse. "You have my undivided attention. So what were we talking about?"

"Well, we were talking about Thomas, but really I'd rather not talk about it any more. It just makes me feel sad, and I don't want anything to take away from the excitement that I know I should be feeling right now, you know?"

Jemma was nodding her head. "So, are you nervous?"

"Yes. No. I don't know." Isabella laughed a little. "I guess I am. Or I will be. How could I not be? I'm meeting my birth father."

"I think it's great, Bella. I mean, of course it's really sad that you never got to meet Arianna, but it must feel good to think about meeting someone else who is your own flesh and blood—about meeting your father." Jemma looked down for a second and Isabella thought she saw something cross her friend's face.

"Hey, Jemma. Sorry, this must be hard for you. I know you don't talk about it much but if you ever want to—talk about your father, I mean—you know I'm here for you."

Isabella knew the whole story about Jemma's family—that Jemma's father wasn't a good guy and that Jemma seemed to have no desire to meet him. Isabella guessed that she was far better off without knowing him, from everything she'd heard about the guy.

"Oh, don't be silly. I'm okay never knowing that guy.

He's no father to me. Chase is the only dad I need. Having him in our lives is the best thing that ever happened to us. But we're not talking about me right now anyway." She reached over to put her hand on Isabella's arm. "Hey, I feel bad for not going with you. It seems like you should have some moral support or something."

Isabella thought about her friend's words carefully. She didn't want to make Jemma feel guilty, but she'd long since promised herself that she was done not being honest about her true feelings.

She reached over to give Jemma a quick hug. "You're so sweet. Don't feel bad. I know you'd come if you were able to. Would it be nice to have someone there to help calm my nerves? Sure. But you know—I'm learning how to do a lot of things on my own, I guess. Real world and all that jazz, huh?" She grinned and when she looked over at her friend, Jemma had a funny but happy look on her face.

Isabella felt hands across her eyes—hands that she thought she recognized. She smiled instinctively as her own hands came to land on the arms that she knew so well, at the same time as she stood up to spin around.

"Thomas!" Without second-guessing anything about how she was feeling, she wrapped her arms around his neck, breathing in the scent of his cologne, trying to hold back her tears at how happy she was to see him. "You came to see me off. You have no idea how happy that makes me." She took a step back to look at him, speaking quickly now and noticing Jemma's grin as she seemed to be making eye contact with Thomas. "Please let's not have any more weirdness between us. I hate it so much."

Thomas pulled her to his chest and kissed her on the top of the head. "I hate it too, Iz. I'm sorry." He pulled away a bit to look her in the eye. "Do you forgive me?"

Isabella nodded, wiping away her tears with one hand.

"But I do want to be clear about something that you're very wrong about."

Thomas's face was suddenly very serious looking.

"Okay…" Isabella took in a deep breath.

"I am not here to see you off."

Isabella was confused as she looked from Thomas to Jemma, who was still grinning like the cat who'd swallowed the canary.

"Thomas?" She grinned at him as she finally noticed the backpack that he had slung over one shoulder.

Thomas shrugged. "I didn't think you should do this trip alone. I figured some moral support might be in order and since I have been a real jerk to you, I'm hoping it will score me some major brownie points."

Isabella flung herself back into Thomas's arms. "Oh, you have no idea how happy this makes me." She looked over at Jemma, who was getting up from her chair. "And you! You were in on this big surprise, weren't you?"

Jemma laughed, coming over to hug Isabella and then Thomas. "He made me promise not to tell. It's a good surprise, huh?"

"It's the best surprise." Isabella squeezed Thomas's arm. "We have a lot of catching up to do, don't we?"

"Yes—I want to know all about this new man in your life. What was his name? Colin? Jemma filled me in with a bit more than I got from you the other day." He winked.

Isabella shot a look toward Jemma just as she was about to walk away. "Jemma!"

"Oh, stop. I didn't tell him anything." She laughed. "Anyway, I'm gonna take off now. Text me when you land, okay, and I'm going to want to know everything—Oh, I'm so excited for you, Bella." Jemma reached over to pull Isabella in for a big hug. "Have the best time and I miss you already."

Thomas was laughing and shaking his head.

"What's so funny?" Jemma asked, laughing a little herself.

"You two. You've been traveling together like twenty-four/seven. Aren't you ready for a break from one another?"

Isabella and Jemma looked at one another and grinned.

"Not really," they said at the same time and then laughed again.

"Jemma is my travel soulmate."

"Really?" Thomas had a fake hurt expression on his face.

"Well, you kinda messed up that position for yourself, didn't you?" Isabella punched him on the arm lightly.

"Yeah, okay. But I'm making up for it now, right?" Thomas leaned over to give a little tug on Isabella's hair.

Jemma shook her head. "You two. Try to behave. Okay, I'm really going now. Have fun."

"Bye, Jem. Big hugs to Blu for me."

Jemma walked away and Isabella eyed Thomas carefully. She really couldn't believe that he was there, sitting next to her—making this trip with her. Thomas had always been there for her when it mattered, and this time it mattered more to her than ever before.

PAULA KAY

CHAPTER 20

Isabella opened her eyes slowly, for a second forgetting that she was on an airplane. Then she saw Thomas sitting next to her—watching her, more accurately. She yawned and then poked him in the arm.

"What are you looking at?"

He grinned. "You. You were snoring."

"Oh, stop. I wasn't."

"Oh, you were. But it was cute. Kinda dainty-like."

Isabella laughed. "Stop teasing me."

"I thought you liked it when I teased you."

"You're right. I do. Don't stop." She watched him for a few seconds.

"Now, what are *you* looking at?"

"Thomas, did something happen between you and Natasha?"

"No, not exactly. Why?"

"Well, it hasn't gone unnoticed by me that you are now sitting on a plane next to me when I'm pretty sure your girlfriend was expecting you to be attending some big wedding with her this weekend."

"True. You're not wrong. And the truth is, she's not happy with me."

"I'll bet she's livid. And not happy with me—that's for sure."

"She'll get over it."

"So, what did you tell her?"

Thomas looked at her, and as they made eye contact it was all she could do to keep from looking away.

"I told her that my best friend needed me—end of story. I told her that I wanted to be there for you and that she just needed to understand that or we were going to be over."

Isabella's heart skipped a beat. Was it possible that everything was going to be normal between them once again?

"You told her that?"

Thomas reached out to take her hand in his. "I did and I meant every word of it, so I hope you're going to be willing to show me a really good time in San Francisco. I put my relationship on the line for this trip."

Isabella punched him on the arm and he laughed.

"Seriously. We're going to have a great time. You'll meet your father—and your sister, Iz. I still can't believe that you have a sister."

Isabella grinned. "I know. Me either. And I want you to meet them also. We'll all have Thanksgiving together. They know you're with me and they seem very welcoming."

"That sounds great. And then I figure if you want to, we'll do a little touring of the city and maybe some shopping if you're up for it. I hear that downtown San Francisco is supposed to be beautiful this time of year."

"Perfect. And we'll talk more about Natasha later." Isabella laid her head back against the seat feeling a bit nervous still, but more content now that Thomas was there with her, making plans with her for this city that would be new and exciting. There was a lot to look forward to.

She was ready for this next stop in her journey.

Thomas whistled as she came out of her dressing room.

They'd checked into their suites at their very fancy hotel near Union Square and had about an hour to rest before Isabella knew that it was time to get ready to meet her father.

She did a little twirl in the simple black dress she'd bought while shopping in Dublin. "Do you like? It's not too much, is it?"

"No, Iz. It's perfect and you look lovely."

Isabella walked over to sit on the small sofa by him. "I'm nervous. Really nervous."

"You'll be fine. It's going to be great."

"How can you be so sure?"

"Because you've told me so many times how great

this man is and that you seemed to have an instant connection over video chat."

"Well, yeah, but that's video chat. This is real life."

"And I'm sure it's going to be that much better. Try not to put any pressure on yourself. It's just your dad tonight, right? Downstairs?"

Isabella nodded. "Yeah, we're just going to have dinner together here tonight. He thought it best if I met the rest of the family tomorrow."

"I think it's nice that it's just the two of you. Unless you want me to come with?" Thomas winked at her.

"No, I know I need to do this on my own. But promise me you'll wait up for me. You can hang out in here if you like. Watch movies or whatever. Thomas, what are you going to do tonight? Is this going to be terribly boring for you?"

He laughed. "I'm ordering in pizza and watching movies. And no, it's not going to be boring at all. I will stay in here to wait for you, and you'll probably find me asleep on your sofa when you get in. Hey, aren't you sleepy too?"

"Kinda, now that you mention it. But I did sleep on the plane, and now I think I'm just too hyper to be sleepy. What time is it?"

Thomas picked up his phone from the coffee table. "Time for you to get going, my darling. It's seven o'clock on the dot."

Isabella stood up. "Shoot. Okay, I gotta go. Wish me

luck."

Thomas stood up too and kissed her on the cheek. "You don't need luck. Just be yourself. He's going to adore you, Iz—the same way everyone does."

"You're too sweet to me."

"I know. You're right. I might deserve many back massages later." He laughed and shoved her gently toward the door. "Go."

"I'm going. Okay. Deep breaths. I'm sure I won't be late." She turned back toward him just before she walked out the door. "Thanks again, Thomas, for coming—and for everything."

"You're welcome. Now, go!"

CHAPTER 21

When Isabella stepped off the elevator she saw Lucas right away. He was standing near some seats just outside of the restaurant. He was tall and dressed in a suit jacket. He looked just as he did on video chat, only so much better in real life. She could hardly believe she was about to meet her father; she started walking toward him before his eyes had yet to find her.

And then he turned and as their eyes met for the first time in person he took a few long strides toward her. He scooped her up into his arms as if she was his four-year-old daughter and not his nearly twenty-year-old daughter.

She laughed as she felt him lift her.

"Oh, Isabella."

She felt his kisses on the top of her head, his hands stroking her hair before he put her down.

"Let me look at you."

Tears were streaking down his face and he didn't bother to brush them away.

Isabella smiled. "It's good to finally meet you."

He pulled her in for a big hug, this time allowing her

feet to stay on the floor.

"Oh, you have no idea how good it is to hold you in my arms. I can't believe this day has finally come. It feels like forever. But now you're here. And there's so much to talk about, isn't there?"

Isabella nodded, feeling a little tongue-tied as she looked at the similarities between them. Lucas had told her so many times how much she looked like Arianna— like her mother—but she knew that she also had her father's features. It was surreal to be looking at him now and she wasn't quite sure how to take it all in.

"You must be hungry. Let's get a table—there will be plenty of time for talking."

He placed his hand gently at the small if her back to guide her into the restaurant as they followed the hostess to their table.

They placed their orders with the waitress and Lucas reached for her hand across the table. "Tell me—how was your flight? You must be pretty exhausted. I won't keep you late."

"I'm doing alright. I slept a bit on the plane. But even if I'm a little tired, it's so surreal to be here—with you, I mean. I wanted to say in person that I'm sorry for the shock of everything you must have felt when Douglas first contacted you about me. I can only imagine what that must have been like—and for your wife."

"You don't need to be sorry for anything. I was surprised but the news was always good, Isabella. I never for one moment was sorry to hear about you. And Kate—you'll meet her tomorrow. She's just the best and will welcome you with open arms. She knew about Arianna, but it was so long ago—way before I met her. I was so young then. It still feels strange that Arianna died so young."

Isabella thought about her next question instead of just blurting it out. She realized that she did still have so many questions—maybe questions that only this man sitting across from her could answer.

"What is it? You can say anything to me, you know? Please. I want you to be yourself. I want to know what you're thinking and feeling. It's the only way that we can truly get to know one another, I think. And I want that. So much."

Isabella smiled. He was so kind—her father. And everything about him was sincere.

"Will you tell me about her—about my mother?"

The waitress came with their food and Isabella spent the next hour listening to her father tell her about a side of Arianna that seemed to be just a touch unlike what she'd learned from the others.

He talked about school dances and county fairs, movie dates and making out in the back of his car. He told her that Arianna had made him laugh like no one else could, even still. And he also told her that she'd broken his heart when he'd been madly in love with her.

Months before Isabella had been born, Arianna had

broken up with him, not giving him a good reason except to say that she was going away to school. She wanted to start fresh, she'd said, without a boyfriend to tie her down. He'd tried to get a hold of her, more times than he could count, but she never would accept his calls. And when he'd found out that she'd returned home, he'd shown up many times at her door, only to be turned away by her parents or, more often than not, Gigi.

Finally he'd given up, and years later when he'd heard, first about her parents, and then about Arianna's passing, it had almost been more than he could bear. It had taken him many months to get over it all—to move on with his own life.

Isabella watched him as he told her these things about her mother, and it was as if all the missing pieces were being put into place one by one. She never tired hearing the stories about her—the good and the not so good—she wanted to know it all.

Now she dared to ask him the question that had been on her mind since the day Douglas had told her that he'd found her father.

"Can I ask you a question?"

"Sure. Ask me anything, Isabella. I mean it."

"What would you have done? If things had been different and you'd known that Arianna had been pregnant?"

Lucas put down the bite of food that he'd been about to put in his mouth and lifted his glass of wine to his lips.

He seemed to be studying Isabella carefully before he answered her.

"I've asked myself that same question—ever since I got that call from Douglas and found out about you. The truth is, Isabella, I don't know what I would have done. I don't know what would have happened. I'd like to say that I would have proposed to your mother, that I'd have been ready to be a father, but when I think about the boy I was then, I'm just not so sure."

Isabella nodded. She appreciated his honestly and hadn't really expected a different answer.

"I do think that I would have supported her—had I known about the pregnancy. I'd have wanted to try to make it work—I really loved her. But the truth is, I never thought she loved me half as much as I loved her. So, I think that she wouldn't have wanted to marry me, to raise a child with me."

Isabella didn't say anything for a few minutes. There were so many thoughts swirling in her head—Arianna's words to her in the journal, all the memories she had as a child being raised by parents who'd loved her so completely.

"It's kind of funny how things work out sometimes, I guess."

She could see the question on Lucas's face.

"I mean, Arianna wrote me in a letter that maybe everything had worked out for the best—that even though she'd not wanted to give me up, I'd been raised by loving parents and it meant that I didn't have to deal with losing her—the way that a daughter would have had to deal with such a thing."

"I can see her point, and I'm also really sorry for the shock that you must have felt. I know we've talked about that before but it's good to know that you don't have any bad feelings toward your parents."

"Well, it wasn't easy at first. That's for sure. But once I understood that they were there to support me and help me when it came to finding out information about Arianna, then everything changed."

"I'm glad. You have no idea how wonderful it makes me feel to know that you're leading a good life—that you're happy."

"Yes, well, it's all a journey, isn't it?" Isabella yawned.

"Oh, look at you. You must be tired. You go on up to bed. I'll just get the bill."

They both stood up.

"It's so nice meeting you. Thank you for dinner," said Isabella.

Lucas hugged her close. "The pleasure is truly all mine. So before you go, we should talk about tomorrow. Kate says to come over any time after one, if that works for you? I can give you the address or I'm happy to come pick you up. We're not far from here—about fifteen minutes with no traffic."

"That sounds perfect, and no need to pick us up, we'll get a taxi. Oh, I did tell you that my friend was with me, didn't I?" Everything had happened so fast that she was now wondering if she'd imagined sending a text to Lucas about Thomas.

Lucas was nodding his head. "Yes, you did tell me, and Kate says the more the merrier. I'll just text you the address then. Oh, and be aware, there's a little girl who is very excited to meet you."

"Annie." Isabella loved the name. It seemed sweet, just how she imagined her younger sister to be. "You tell her that I can't wait to play with her."

They hugged one last time and then Isabella started back to her room for a quick chat with Thomas, who was hopefully still awake, and then a much-needed night's sleep.

She was very happy, and suddenly, very exhausted.

PAULA KAY

CHAPTER 22

Isabella watched out the window of the taxi as she and Thomas made their way to where Lucas lived in Pacific Heights. She felt much less nervous after meeting him last night and she was mostly very excited to meet Annie—and to see where they lived.

"I'm really glad that your meeting went so well last night," said Thomas. "Today should be fun."

"Thanks for coming with me." Isabella smiled at him. "After today, we'll take some time to do the things that you want to do while we're here."

"I'm not worried about that. This trip is all about you, my darling."

"San Francisco is really beautiful, isn't it? Just look at those views."

They were coming to the top of another hill, and the water with the Golden Gate Bridge in the background was breathtaking.

Isabella pointed. "I think that must be Sausalito over there—where Arianna lived."

"Do you want to go there? We should try to find out

the address."

"I thought about asking Gigi and Douglas, but I know the house was sold several years ago now. I think maybe it's enough to just be here—near where she lived, you know? I would definitely like to go for a walk across the bridge. Gigi and Blu have told me many times how much my mother loved to do that."

Thomas reached out to touch her arm. "We'll do that tomorrow if you like."

Isabella continued to stare out the window, lost in thoughts about a young Arianna driving these same streets in the red convertible that she'd heard so much about.

When the taxi pulled up to a big three-story house on top of one of the hills, Isabella saw a young girl peek out the window and then disappear behind the curtain, only to come running out the front door toward them a few seconds later.

As Thomas paid the driver, Lucas appeared in the doorway with a big grin on his face.

The little girl ran over to Isabella, wrapping her arms around her waist. "I'm Annie." She looked up at Isabella and grinned. "You're my sister."

Isabella laughed and bent down so that she was eye-to-eye with the little girl. "It's so nice to finally meet you, Annie. And I feel so lucky to have you for a sister."

"I'm four."

"Well, you're a big girl, aren't you?" Isabella smiled

and gestured to Thomas, who had walked over next to them. "This is my friend Thomas."

"Hi Thomas." Annie stuck her hand out and Isabella and Thomas both burst out laughing.

"Well, aren't you a polite little girl."

Lucas walked over to Isabella, giving her a big hug.

He stuck out his hand toward Thomas. "Lucas. It's great to meet you, Thomas. Welcome to our home. Shall we go inside?"

Annie reached for Isabella's hand.

They followed Lucas through the doorway into the foyer. Isabella could see a beautifully decorated living room with a set dining table in the room just beyond it. A woman, who could only be Lucas's wife Kate, came walking toward them, wiping her hands on the apron she wore.

She wrapped her arms around Isabella's neck in a big hug. "Isabella, it's so great to finally meet you." She pulled away to look at her. "I hope you don't mind. I'm a hugger." She laughed and studied Isabella for a few seconds before turning toward Lucas. "You're right, honey, she's very beautiful."

Lucas laughed. "That, of course, is her mother's Italian genes."

"And you must be Thomas?" Kate stepped over to where Thomas stood, giving him a big hug as well. "We're just so happy to have you both here."

"Well, something sure does smell fantastic," said

Thomas, rubbing his stomach. "We skipped eating a big breakfast this morning, in preparation."

Kare laughed. "Come sit down. Let me get you something to drink."

They followed Kate into the living room, Annie close by Isabella's side.

"Wanna come see my room? You too, Thomas," said Annie.

Isabella looked over toward Kate, who'd come back in with the water they'd requested.

"Oh, go ahead. I think the food will be ready by the time you come back down. Then we can all have a nice big chat around the table. I've made enough food to keep us busy eating for hours."

Isabella and Thomas followed the excited Annie up the staircase. She was singing a song for them and when she wasn't singing she was talking a mile a minute.

Isabella looked over at Thomas and mouthed the words "my sister." She thought Annie was adorable, and she nearly had to pinch herself to remind her that she was a big sister now.

They let Annie give them the tour of her room, which included her pink canopy bed, her huge dollhouse, her corner stage and dressing area, and a closet full of the costumes that she said her mother made for her.

By the time Kate called them down to eat twenty minutes later, Isabella, Thomas, and Annie were fast friends. This time it was Thomas's hand the little girl held as they made their way down the stairs to the kitchen.

Isabella walked behind them smiling to herself as she watched Thomas with her little sister. He really was going to make a great father one day. He had just the right balance of playfulness and common sense—and he was always so gentle. It was a word that often came to her mind to describe her best friend, and now as she saw him brush Annie's hair out of her eyes, the sweetness of it almost made her tear up.

They made their way into the dining room and laughed when Annie positioned herself right between them at the table.

"Honey, maybe Isabella and Thomas would like to sit next to each other," said Lucas as he patted the seat next to him. "Why don't you come sit over here across from Isabella?"

"Oh, no. You're fine right where you are, right, Thomas?" Isabella said, smiling.

"Certainly. I'd love to sit next to you. I can sit next to Isabella any old time."

They all laughed and Kate set the turkey on the table.

"Kate, that looks amazing. Thank you so much for going to all the trouble," said Isabella.

"Oh, it's not trouble at all. This is one of our favorite days of the year, right, Annie?"

Annie nodded. "Yep, it's when we give thanks for everything we have and all the people we love." She turned to look at Isabella, for the first time appearing to be just slightly shy in her demeanor. "Know what, Isabella?"

"What, Annie?" Isabella laughed lightly.

"I love you now too." Annie grinned

Isabella felt instant tears and she saw Lucas wiping at his own eyes across the table too. She leaned down to kiss the top of Annie's head. "I love you too and I'm so happy to finally have a sister."

Thomas smiled over the little girl's head at Isabella and she thought again how incredible it was that he'd come with her.

The meal was delicious—everything Isabella loved in a Thanksgiving feast—and the conversation flowed easily. She really liked Kate and the feel of being with them all in their home. There'd been no awkwardness at all, and Isabella felt as if she'd known them for years.

Annie had fallen asleep after lunch while watching a video, and the grown-ups were enjoying coffee and dessert out on the patio. Isabella had had quite a nice chat while helping Kate clean up in the kitchen, and now she watched her interact with Lucas as the four of them laughed and told stories. They seemed to have a very loving easy marriage, often finishing one another's sentences and not shy with their affection at all.

Isabella laughed with Lucas and Kate as Thomas told them funny stories about Isabella's childhood. He reached over to tug at her hair and pull her in for a quick hug.

"So how long have you two been together then?" Kate asked.

Isabella felt her face go warm, which was ridiculous. She looked at Thomas and laughed. "Oh, we're just friends."

"Well, come on now. We're not *just* friends," Thomas laughed when Isabella looked at him with what she was sure was a very confused expression. He reached over to take her hand. "Izzy's the best friend I've ever had." He looked across the table at Lucas and Kate. "That's seriously the truth. Iz is an amazing person. You'll be glad to know her."

Isabella punched him lightly in the arm. "Gee, talk about a love fest. Thanks for that, Thomas." She really hoped that she wasn't blushing as much as she thought she might be.

Lucas and Kate started laughing at the same time.

"Well, everyone should be as lucky to have such a good friend," said Kate.

"I concur," said Lucas.

PAULA KAY

CHAPTER 23

Isabella reached over to the nightstand to get her phone, which had dinged with an incoming text. She and Thomas had gotten home from Lucas's about a half hour ago and decided that they'd rest for a little while and then go out for a small meal. The day had been beyond incredible. She'd enjoyed every minute, and they'd made plans to all have one more meal out together before she left town.

She looked down at the text on her phone and sat straight up in bed. It was from Douglas.

Surprise! Gigi and I are in town. Call me?

She punched in a response.

You're in San Francisco??!

We are. Can I call you?

Yes, please.

Her phone buzzed a second later.

"Douglas? What are you two doing here and why didn't you tell me you were coming?"

She heard him laughing on the other end of the phone.

"Well, we weren't sure about it until a few days ago. Gigi had some family in town who really wanted us to come spend the holiday with them and we were able to get a few days covered at the orphanage, which wasn't easy with our big Christmas trip coming up too."

"Well, I want to see you guys. Oh, and Thomas is with me. I really want you to meet."

"Well, that's partly why I'm calling. I have a surprise that you might like."

"I do like surprises." Isabella laughed.

"I think I mentioned to you that it was a buddy of mine that ended up buying the Sausalito house from us. When I found out that we were going to be here at the same time as you, I gave him a call. It turns out they're out of town but he said that he'd be more than happy for me to let us in so that I could show you the house where Arianna lived."

Isabella couldn't speak. Tears rolled down her cheeks as she listened to what Douglas was telling her. It seemed an unreal possibility, yet it was one of the last missing pieces to knowing more about her birth mother.

"Bella, are you there?"

It was Gigi's voice in her ear now.

"Are you okay, honey? I can't wait to see you."

"Sorry." Isabella tried to force the words out. "It will be so nice to see you, Gigi. And the house. I can't believe I'm going to get to see it."

"I know, honey. I'm so happy that we get a chance to

show it to you. We'll make a nice day of it, okay? I'm going to put Douglas back on so that you can work out the details."

"Okay."

"Sorry. I know this is a little unexpected—hopefully in a good way."

"Yes, its very good news. You have no idea how happy you're making me right now. First meeting my father and now this."

"Gigi and I want to hear all about that meeting when we see you, by the way. So will tomorrow work for you then? We've got a driver while we're here, so we could pick you up around ten? And then after we see the house, we'll all have lunch together. Thomas too, of course."

"That sounds perfect. I can't wait to see you both tomorrow. Give Gigi a kiss for me."

Isabella clicked off the phone and then called Thomas.

"Hello?"

"Sorry. Are you awake?"

"Am now." He laughed into the phone. "Are you hungry already?"

"Oh no. Not really. But I do have some news that I'm very excited about." She felt herself grinning just talking about it. "Can you come down to my room?"

"Sure. Give me ten minutes."

She filled Thomas in on the plans for the next day.

They ordered a pizza, deciding a good night's sleep was more important than a night out. Thomas had been excited for her, and seemed very pleased to be able to share in all of these firsts that were happening for Isabella in relation to her family and who Arianna had been.

By the time Isabella went to bed, her head was swimming with thoughts of Lucas, Annie, Kate—and now this big piece of her birth mother's history that was going to be opened up to her. She made a mental note to phone Jemma in the morning as well as her parents later on in the day.

It was important to her that she keep her parents in the loop about everything that had been going on. She'd texted them to wish them a happy Thanksgiving and to tell them everything had gone well with Lucas, but she needed for them to hear her voice as well.

Finally she felt herself drifting off to sleep, with good thoughts about seeing Gigi and Douglas the next day and what it would mean for all of them to be together in the house across the bridge.

CHAPTER 24

Isabella sat on the window seat in Arianna's bedroom, looking at Douglas and Thomas, who were sitting outside in the garden. Gigi sat on the small sofa just opposite her, and Isabella didn't miss the tears in her eyes as she watched her. She turned around to face Gigi.

"You look just like her, you know, Bella. I can picture Ari sitting there right now—just as you are—and it plays with my mind a bit, if I'm being honest. We had many chats sitting up here." Gigi traced a finger along the edge of the sofa. "Douglas and I included all of the furniture with the sale of the house, and I must say how pleased I am that they've not changed this room."

"I'm sorry if it's painful for you to be here, Gigi." Isabella crossed to sit beside Gigi on the small sofa. "We don't have to stay long."

"No. Don't be silly. This day and this visit is all about you." Gigi reached over to take Isabella's hand in hers. "I love it that you're here. It sends chills up and down my spine to think what Ari would have thought about you being here. I think it would have made her very happy."

"I think so too." Isabella smiled and then went back to the window seat. "I wonder what those two are talking about out there." She could see Thomas laughing below as Douglas appeared to be pointing something out in the distance.

"I'm glad we finally get to meet your Thomas, by the way."

Isabella looked at Gigi when she spoke, not missing the amused look on her face. Her Thomas. It was a funny way to describe a best friend. She laughed.

"Well, I'm not so sure that he's *my* Thomas— especially if his new girlfriend has anything to say about it—but I am really glad that you got to meet him. He's been a big part of my life for so many years."

"It's important to have people like that in your life," said Gigi. "I hope the two of you will guard that incredible friendship you have—don't let anything come between you, even significant others." She winked and Isabella laughed.

"Time will tell. Right now everything is fine, but I think when he gets back to London, he's going to have a lot of making up to do."

She'd already filled Gigi in just briefly about Thomas's decision to come to San Francisco with her. Gigi had said that he was a true keeper for recognizing what that would mean to Isabella.

Gigi stood up from the sofa. "I'm going to go downstairs and see what the boys are up to. Do you want a little time to yourself here?"

Isabella nodded. "Yeah, I'd like that. I won't be long."

"Take your time, Bella."

Isabella got up to walk around the bedroom to the bathroom. She looked at herself in the mirror, imagining Arianna getting ready for a night out or taking a bath in the big tub. Gigi had told her that it had been one of Arianna's favorite things to do—to relax in a big bubble bath.

She walked back out to the window seat again, thinking about her mother looking out over the very same view of the Golden Gate Bridge in the distance. She'd spent hours in this very seat writing in her journal or poring over the world map that Isabella now kept so carefully with her at all times. It was easy to imagine Arianna here. It was easy to imagine herself doing so many of those same kinds of things. She wished that her mother would have known those things about her.

Isabella took one last look around the room before she headed downstairs and out to the garden where everyone was sitting, deep in conversation that included lots of laughter.

"Is this where you two got married, Gigi?" said Isabella.

Gigi and Douglas looked at one another.

"It is, yes," said Gigi, a broad smile on her face.

"It's also where I first met my lovely bride." Douglas reached over to touch Gigi's face.

Isabella had heard the whole story about how Douglas had been best friends with Gigi's employer, Arianna's adoptive father—about how they'd known one another for years and how Arianna had been so sure that they belonged together. It was really wonderful to hear the stories and to see them back where it had all begun.

She stood up to walk to the edge of the garden, feeling Thomas's arm come around her shoulders as he came to stand beside her.

"How are you doing, Iz? Does it feel good for you to be here? Or does it feel weird at all?"

Isabella looked over at him and smiled. "Good—only good. It feels pretty incredible, really—like so many of my questions have been answered now, I'm not sure that I have many left."

Thomas grinned at her. "That's a good thing, right?"

Isabella nodded and then turned back toward Gigi and Douglas. "We can go whenever you're ready." She walked over to give them both a big hug. "Thank you again so much for making this happen."

"You're welcome, honey," said Douglas. "I'm happy that it all worked out the way it did."

"And we're especially happy that we got to see our Isabella," said Gigi, giving Isabella a big squeeze.

"I know. And I get to see you again next month. I can hardly wait for Christmas in Tuscany this year."

CHAPTER 25

Gigi and Douglas had stayed back near the parking lot when they made the stop at the Golden Gate Bridge so that Isabella and Thomas could walk it. At their lunch spot in Sausalito, Isabella had mentioned to them that it was something she'd like to do and now she and Thomas were taking the walk across it.

Isabella shivered and Thomas put his arm around her.

"It is cold, isn't it?" Thomas said.

"Yes, I wish I'd brought my stocking cap with me. I had no idea."

"Give me your hand." Thomas took her hand in his, blowing on first one and then the other, before he kept hers nestled in his own with a squeeze.

"Maybe going to the center will be good enough." Isabella laughed. "I also don't want to keep Gigi and Douglas waiting too long."

"They're really great, by the way. And they sure do love you." Thomas grinned at her.

"Yeah, I really love them too. It's kind of strange how

I could feel so connected to people that I've really not spent that much time with."

"It's your mother. That's where the connection comes from. Heck, after hearing all the stories and seeing her home, I feel kinda connected to Arianna myself."

Isabella laughed. "Do you?"

"Well, I feel like you've changed a lot since everything happened—since you've met everyone and found out so much about your mother." He must have noticed the question on Isabella's face. "For the better, I mean—always for the better, Iz." He laughed. "You just seem more content. There's a certain peace about you and for that I'm really grateful. I can't help but wonder if it was Arianna's intention to give you that gift—if that makes sense?"

Isabella was quiet for several seconds as they came to a stop at the center of the bridge. She reached into her purse to pull out the small wrapped urn of Arianna's ashes. She'd always been alone before in the various places that she'd let them go, but having Thomas here with her now felt somehow right. She wanted to share it with him.

Thomas looked at the object but he didn't say anything. He put his arm around her shoulders and leaned over to kiss her head as she pulled one of the small bags of ashes from the urn.

She looked over at him. "I've been doing this in every place. Well, it has been every place that Arianna had on her map—the places that she'd dreamed of going. It's made me feel even more connected to her somehow—like we've been on this journey together."

Thomas reached over to wipe away the few tears that had made their way down her cheeks. "I think that's beautiful."

He swallowed hard, and Isabella was touched at the emotion that she felt from him.

"Her ashes have already been let go here—by everyone else—because they knew how much she loved the bridge and this city, but somehow it feels fitting that I should do it here too, doesn't it?"

Thomas nodded his head and moved his arm from Isabella's shoulders to her waist, pulling her close to him. "It feels perfect."

They stood there quietly for a few minutes after Isabella had discreetly emptied the small bag over the water below. The sun shone brightly now and the skyline of the city in the distance was breathtaking to Isabella. It was as beautiful, if not more so, than any of the places she'd traveled to so far.

Thomas was watching her; she could feel it before she even turned toward him. But she wasn't ready to speak just yet. The silence was comfortable to her—standing there, where her mother had stood so many years ago—it felt oddly perfect to Isabella and for a moment she was reluctant to leave. She took a deep breath in and closed her eyes, wanting to seal the memory of the place and the moment forever.

Finally, she opened her eyes and glanced over at Thomas. "We should be getting back to Gigi and Douglas."

"Okay, are you ready?"

She nodded and they started walking back where they'd come from.

It had been a good day, one that Isabella would always remember. It felt like things had come full circle—her being in the place where Arianna had taken her last breath. She reached out to take Thomas's hand. "Gigi and Douglas are leaving tomorrow."

"And us the day after already. It's gone fast, huh?"

"Too fast. So I was thinking maybe I'd see if we could move our dinner plans with Lucas and Kate to a morning brunch—Kate told me they were totally flexible. And that would give you and me the rest of the day to do some sightseeing or shopping—whatever we feel like."

"You can spend the day with them if you want to, Iz. I don't mind."

Isabella shook her head. "No, I'll see them once more, but then I want to spend the time with you here. You deserve it, remember? Before you get back to the wrath." Isabella laughed, but then noticed the stern look Thomas was giving her. "Oops. I'm sorry. Disregard that last statement."

Thomas laughed. "I'm only joking. And you're kinda right. But I've talked to Natasha a few times since I've been here and I think everything's going to be okay."

"Well, good. I don't have to feel so guilty then." Isabella grinned.

Thomas looked over at her and smiled as they walked back into the parking lot where Gigi and Douglas were waiting for them. "You don't have to feel guilty at all."

PAULA KAY

CHAPTER 26

Isabella leaned against Thomas as they waited for the cable car to come to a stop near Union Square. Earlier that morning, they'd met Lucas, Kate and Annie for breakfast at a restaurant near Fisherman's Wharf, and they'd all spent some time walking around playing tourist for a few hours. It had been a bit difficult when the time had come to say goodbye, especially to Annie—who started crying and wouldn't stop until Isabella promised her that they'd do video calls with one another every week.

Thomas hopped off the cable car, reaching out his hand for Isabella to take as she hopped off behind him.

"So, where to, my lady?"

"Didn't you say that you had some Christmas shopping to do? We could go over to where the shops are on Union Square, and also you might want my help if by Christmas shopping you mean shopping for Natasha?" Isabella laughed.

"Yes and yes. I actually have no idea what to get her, but…"

"But what?"

"Oh, nothing."

Isabella stopped walking. "Thomas, what? Don't keep things from me—not after the great time we've been having together."

"Okay. I was just thinking that I'm not sure that anything other than a ring would really make her happy."

"Well, that is tricky then, isn't it?"

"Meaning?"

"Meaning, I'm not so sure that I'm ready to help you shop for an engagement ring."

For Natasha.

"Hey, I'm not so sure that *I'm* ready to be shopping for an engagement ring, so how about if we don't do that." Thomas laughed.

"But I can help you find her something else. If you want me to?"

"Yes. Let's do that."

They walked into one of the fancier shops and started looking at jewelry.

"Does she wear a lot of jewelry?"

"She does, yes. She has a lot, actually."

"Ooh, I like these." Isabella gazed into the case at several different sets of diamond earrings.

"Do you? Which ones do you like?" Thomas studied her with a thoughtful expression on his face. "Do you even ever wear jewelry, Iz?"

Isabella shrugged. "No, but if I did wear jewelry, I'd

want to wear diamonds." She laughed. "But I'm not really the diamond-wearing kinda girl, am I?"

Thomas leaned back against the jewelry case. "Seriously, Iz. What are you talking about? You do realize that you could afford to wear diamonds now?" He winked at her.

Thomas knew the kind of money she'd inherited from Arianna; she had more than enough to buy any type of jewelry she wanted.

"Oh, I don't know. I was kind of joking, but I guess now that we're talking about it, I feel like a certain kind of woman deserves to wear diamonds more than another kind of woman."

"So, you're saying that you're not the kind of woman that deserves it?"

"I guess. I'm probably more of a costume jewelry kinda girl."

Thomas was shaking his head. "Well, I for one think you're very wrong about that. Any of those diamond earrings would look beautiful on you."

"Well, thank you, but we're not shopping for me right now; so what do you think about Natasha?"

"Hmm. I think Natasha is more of a pearl kinda woman."

"Okay." Isabella walked on to look into the next jewelry case.

"But now I'm thinking maybe getting her pearls or any kind of jewelry is a bad idea."

"Why?"

Thomas almost grimaced.

"Oh, right—because any kind of jewelry isn't going to be the engagement ring that's what Natasha really wants."

"Exactly." Thomas looked like he was scanning the store. "So any other ideas?"

"Perfume?"

"Nah, she's pretty particular about the kind she wears."

"How 'bout a nice scarf? A leather handbag?"

"She's got too many purses as it but you just gave me an idea. I'll get her a nice leather planner."

"To plan the wedding." Isabella grinned.

"You're pretty funny." Thomas tapped her lightly on the end of the nose. "Don't think I don't know how to get you back for your teasing."

"Thanks for the warning."

Thomas picked out the planner and then they headed to the escalator.

"So, where are we going?"

"I'm taking you for something you love."

"Does it involve food?"

"Maybe."

"Does it involve chocolate?"

Thomas grinned. "You know me so well."

"If you're taking me for chocolate, I'd say that you know *me* so well." Isabella laughed.

"I heard that there's a cafe at the top of the

department store that serves the most amazing hot chocolate and has views of the square."

"Nice. I'm down with that."

"Oh, I figured you would be." Thomas laughed.

Isabella sipped her hot chocolate, while watching the people below. There was a huge Christmas tree set up in the square and decorations were everywhere—as were people—bustling about with shopping bags and determined looks on their faces.

"Hey, look." Isabella pointed out the window. "There's an ice skating rink."

"It looks a little crazy out there." said Thomas.

"I like it." Isabella grinned.

She'd never really gotten into the post-Thanksgiving Day shopping back home, so it was fun to do it in the city and especially with Thomas. She looked at him now across the table. He looked happy. He looked like she was feeling—content.

"So what are you thinking? What would you like to do the rest of the day?" Thomas asked.

Isabella grinned and gestured below.

"You wanna go ice skating?" Thomas smiled back at her.

It was something they used to do together as kids back home. Isabella had actually been pretty good at one time, and she'd make Thomas practice endlessly with her so that she could finally skate backwards with him and do the slowest of twirls.

She looked at him now as she finished the last of her hot chocolate.

"I do. I do want to go ice skating. And you know what? I was thinking, maybe instead of going out for dinner tonight, let's order in and watch movies?"

Thomas stood up, offering her his hand. "That all sounds like the perfect way to end our San Francisco adventure together."

Isabella smiled in response, but inside, her stomach fell. She didn't want their time together to end. She didn't want to go back to the reality of Natasha and wondering if and when she'd get to hang out with Thomas again after this.

She looked at him walking next to her, so handsome and sure of himself as he led her across the street and through the crowds of people to stand in line to buy their tickets. *Just enjoy today, Isabella.*

He looked back at her and then leaned over to kiss her on the cheek.

Isabella laughed. "What was that for?"

"Oh, I don't know. I'm just really happy to be here with you. And you look so cute with your stocking cap and rosy cheeks."

Isabella was glad that the chill in the air seemed to be hiding her blush. It seemed she was blushing around Thomas a lot lately.

CHAPTER 27

Isabella was laughing as she opened the door to greet Thomas. She had Christmas music playing and a fire going in the fireplace. She'd already ordered their dinner from room service and she'd pulled up one of their favorite comedies on the pay-per-view channel.

Thomas crossed the room and settled himself on one end of the large sofa. "You sure are in a festive spirit." He laughed. "I don't know that I've ever known you to be quite this jolly around the holidays."

"Well, today was really wonderful, wasn't it? I loved all the holiday decorations—and even all the people out and about, as crazy as it was in those crowds today."

"Yeah. You got that right." He pulled one of his sneakers off. "You don't mind, do you?"

"No, go ahead. Make yourself comfortable."

"Well, I figure since you're looking pretty comfortable yourself."

Isabella looked down at her pajama bottoms and sweatshirt and laughed. They'd practically grown up having sleepovers at one another's houses—once her parents had loosened up about being so strict with her. She knew that Thomas was used to seeing her like this and she loved that she didn't have to be any certain way with him.

She plopped down on the sofa next to him. "Well, you know me. I'm always up for a casual movie night."

Thomas looked over at her. "I missed this—us hanging out. Today was really good. I'm glad I came, Iz."

Isabella felt her face growing warm and was thankful for the knock at the door.

"The food!"

Thomas got up from the sofa. "You sit. I'll get it."

"Wow. I think this is the best burger I've ever eaten." Isabella sat back against the sofa, her hand on her stomach. "I'm stuffed."

"You don't mean that." Thomas had a funny look of shock on his face. "Better than the diner? Better than *our* diner?"

"Well, no. Not better than the diner, I guess." Isabella eyed him carefully, unsure if she should ask what was on her mind.

"What? What it is?"

"Do you and Natasha eat burgers together?"

Thomas looked at her with an odd expression on his face. "What made you ask that?"

She could sense his body tense a bit at the question and she instantly regretted it. "Oh, I was just wondering. Never mind. It doesn't matter."

"I think maybe we shouldn't talk about Natasha."

Isabella shook her head. "You're right. Sorry. I shouldn't have brought it up. We've had such a good day and—"

"—No. Natasha doesn't eat red meat. And she hates diners, actually." Thomas looked at her and then laughed.

"What? What's so funny?"

"I found this diner a couple blocks away from where we live. She doesn't know that I've been going there—she's trying to get me to quit eating meat too." Thomas wrinkled his nose.

"So you've been sneaking away to the diner?" Isabella laughed.

He looked like a little kid sharing a big dark secret as he nodded his head in reply—just like how they used to share secrets.

"So, how full are you really, Iz?" Thomas was eyeing the last covered plate on the table in front of them. "I know what you've got there."

"You think you know me so well, do you?"

"Oh, yes. I know that when I take off that cover, I'm going to find one chocolate brownie with nuts—and whipped cream, as I'm sure they have it here—and one piece of cheesecake with strawberry sauce." He reached down to unveil what he'd guessed correctly as Isabella laughed.

"Shall I do the honors?" Thomas picked up the knife and Isabella nodded her head as she reached for her fork.

"You shall."

He handed her a plate with half the brownie and half the cheesecake and then settled back into the sofa with his own.

She grinned at him.

"Now what?"

"Nothing."

"What?"

"I miss this."

"Sharing dessert together?"

She looked him in the eye after swallowing a big bite of brownie. "I miss us."

Thomas looked back at her. "Me too, Iz."

Isabella cleared the dishes and food away from the coffee table, grabbing the nearby blanket and remote control, before settling back on the sofa beside Thomas. "Ready to start the movie?"

Thomas patted his stomach. "Yep, totally ready to veg out. We can do the popcorn later."

She gave him a look and he laughed. "Popcorn? No way. Not tonight."

"Just kidding. I'm stuffed too. Let's watch the movie."

Isabella hit play and spread the blanket across her lap, holding it out for Thomas. "Want some?"

He took it, stretching it across both of them as they watched the movie, cracking up in all the same places that they'd done so many times before as they'd watched the same movie together back home. "This is great, Iz. Just like old times, huh?"

"Yeah." Isabella said as she yawned.

"Tired?"

"A little, but I'm okay." She yawned again.

"Come here." Thomas grabbed one of the small throw pillows and pulled her head down on his lap.

Isabella's heart was beating so quickly. It felt strange to be so close to him, but at the same time it felt so right. She felt his hand on her hair and then resting on her shoulder. She could smell his cologne and it was all she could do to resist turning towards him—nestling her face into his chest and falling asleep there, but it was Thomas—Thomas, her best friend.

Isabella's phone buzzed from the table with an incoming video call. Thomas leaned over to pick it up. "It's Colin."

She couldn't be sure but she thought she saw something flash across his face as he gently pushed her up off his lap.

"Go ahead. We can pause the movie."

Isabella didn't take the time to think about it, grabbing her phone to head toward her bedroom. "No. Don't pause it. It's okay. I won't be long."

She saw Thomas nod his head as she answered the

call and then walked into her bedroom.

It was nice to hear from Colin, as it had been a while since they'd spoken, but she was having a hard time concentrating if she was being honest with herself. All she could think about was Thomas in the other room and the nice feeling of being so close to him. She shook her head as if doing so would rid her mind of such thoughts. She hung up the call after five minutes, ending with the promise to call him back the next day, and then left her phone in the bedroom.

Thomas seemed intent on the movie when she went back in to sit next to him. His arms were folded across his chest, the blanket bunched up next to him on the sofa. He looked over at her when she sat down. "How's Colin?"

"Oh, he's fine. He just wanted to know how everything was going—with my father and all."

"Mm-hm." Thomas's attention was back on the movie.

"What, Thomas?"

He sighed, looking back at her. "Nothing, Iz." He smiled. "Let's just finish the movie, okay?"

"Sure." Isabella grabbed for the blanket and settled in at the opposite end of the sofa, feeling the distance between them heavy as the blanket she had around her. She willed herself to focus on the movie, but all she wanted was to be closer to Thomas again. If only she'd left her phone off… If only…what? What exactly did she want or expect to happen? These were crazy thoughts—thoughts that she shouldn't be having—not about Thomas.

As if reading her mind, Thomas glanced at her, then reached out to take her hand, pulling her close to him and back down on the pillow still on his lap. He laughed. "You seemed so comfortable earlier."

She nodded her head from where she rested it on the pillow, trying to take quiet deep breaths in the hopes of slowing her racing heart.

"Iz?"

"Yeah?"

"Do you really like that guy?"

"Hm. I dunno."

"What do you mean, you don't know?" Thomas laughed lightly and she felt his hand on her shoulder again.

"I mean, I guess I haven't spent too much time thinking about it. We don't really know one another all that well. Why?"

"He doesn't really seem like your type to me."

Isabella wanted to sit up and look him in the eye. But she didn't. Her heart beat faster again as she wondered exactly where the conversation was going. "And you think you know what my type is?" She laughed lightly, hoping the question sounded like the joke that it wasn't all of the sudden.

You're my type, Thomas. The thought was in her head,

honest and louder than she'd ever heard it before.

Thomas was quiet. She turned her face so that she could see him out of the corner of her eye. His fingers reached to bring the hair back from her eyes—his fingers more gentle than she'd imagined, the look on his face unreadable but a look she didn't think she'd seen before.

He looked like he wanted to say something, but then he just pushed her up gently from his lap once again as the movie credits were rolling on the TV screen. "I should go." He stood up.

"Oh. Okay."

"Our early flight and all," he was saying as he reached for the doorknob. "Thanks, Iz—for the movie, dinner, everything."

She nodded. "It's been fun—a really nice day." She made herself smile, hating that things suddenly felt so awkward between them. *Please don't let it be awkward.*

He reached out to give her a quick hug and then he was gone, leaving Isabella alone with the thoughts that would keep her awake half the night.

CHAPTER 28

Isabella leaned back in her seat as the plane began its ascent, thankful that there'd been no weirdness between her and Thomas that morning. In fact, it was as if nothing at all had happened, the jokes flowing between them, their easy banter in its rightful spot. Okay, so nothing really *had* happened—except maybe in Isabella's head. She'd spent the last several minutes convincing herself that anything she thought she'd felt between them the night before had all been in her head—that it had been just like any other ordinary movie night between them.

Thomas looked at her, then reached out to give her hand a squeeze. "You okay?"

She nodded her head, feeling slightly confused. "Yeah, why?"

"About the flying?" He laughed.

"Oh, right. I know—can you believe it? I'm practically a pro now." She laughed too, thinking about how far she'd come from that young girl who was dead set against ever setting foot on a plane.

Thomas squeezed her hand again before letting it go. "I can believe it. You've changed a lot, Iz." He turned toward her again after looking out the window for a second.

Isabella knew that her confusion probably showed on her face as he did so.

"For the better, I mean. You've come a long away— getting over some fears, not being so strict with yourself. I'm proud of you." He grinned widely and she felt her own smile match his as she let the words sink in.

"Thanks. That means a lot. Really." She felt the tears just behind her eyelids and didn't want Thomas to notice. "Sorry. I guess I didn't get such great sleep last night. I'm going to close my eyes for a few minute."

"Go ahead." Thomas reached for his earbuds. "I'm gonna listen to some tunes and zone out myself."

When Isabella woke up, it took her a full ten seconds to realize where she was. Thomas was there—sitting next to her. She leaned forward a bit in her seat to peer out the window at the sky over the Atlantic.

London. They were on their way back to London after the most amazing whirlwind time away. Thomas was on his way back to Natasha. She hated it that she felt physically sick thinking about it—thinking about the two of them together.

Get a hold of yourself, Isabella. Keep it together and don't start anything. Things are good with Thomas. They need to stay that way.

Thomas stirred a bit next to her, seemingly fast asleep himself. She looked at him for a moment, watching the way his lips parted slightly with each breath that he took. She loved Thomas as a friend—as her best friend. She just needed to keep reminding herself of that and things would be fine.

She had a lot on her mind anyway. Jemma had written her to let her know that the box had arrived. She smiled, thinking about her book and the fact that she'd kept most of it a secret. Only Jemma knew the details and that she was actually already published. She'd done a great job keeping it from Thomas, despite all of his questions about it. He'd be surprised, as would the rest of her family at Christmas.

She grinned. Family. That was what Thomas was to her. He was like the older brother she'd never had. She laughed as Thomas opened his eyes, stirring finally from his sleep. Okay, so maybe convincing herself that he was *just* like a brother was going to take a bit of work. Isabella was apparently still quite good at telling lies to herself.

"Hey, wow. I can't believe I fell asleep. I didn't realize I was so tired." Thomas stretched his arms overhead. "Any idea how much longer?"

"No, but several hours at least." Isabella pulled out her journal from the seat pocket in front of her.

"That's the first time I've seen you with your journal since we've been gone. Still writing in it a lot?"

"Yeah, for the most part. When I'm not worried about hitting my word count goals for the day." She laughed lightly.

"Ah, but this is different than your fiction, right? These are your innermost thoughts and feelings, yes? Something I'm sure that you'd only share with your very best friend in all the world?"

Thomas was teasing her, but Isabella couldn't help but think back to a time not so long ago when Thomas knew all her secrets. There was nothing she'd kept from him. But lately—lately she couldn't say the same. And she'd never risk letting him read what she'd written in her journal the night before—after he'd left her sleepless in her hotel room. Her face grew hot thinking about it.

"Isabella!" Thomas had a fake shocked look on his face. "You do have deep dark secrets in there, don't you?" He winked at her but he was staring at her intently.

"Oh, stop. No. Not really. But no. It's still only for me to read." She laughed, hoping she sounded normal and like she was joking.

"Hmm."

"What?"

"I'm intrigued."

"Thomas! Watch a movie or something." Isabella laughed.

He laughed too, turning the video monitor to the movie selections. "That is actually a great idea. You go ahead writing your profound thoughts while I find some hilariously juvenile comedy to watch."

"Mm-hm. You do that." Isabella pretended to be deep in concentration, her pen poised over the page, while inside she was still cringing at the idea of Thomas reading her journal.

Several written journal pages later, followed by some reading of the novel she'd just picked up for the trip, followed by two movies she'd selected herself to watch, Isabella was relieved to hear the announcement from the pilot that they were getting ready to make their descent into London. She and Thomas both readied their seats and turned off their electronics and then watched out the window as the city below grew closer.

"Are you excited?" Isabella asked.

"To be back? Yeah, sure. I like London. You?"

"Well, I wasn't just taking about London, silly. Are you excited to see Natasha?" Isabella held her breath, hoping it wasn't going to start them into a conversation that would end in an argument. That was the last thing she wanted.

"Sure."

"Is she meeting you at the airport?"

"Yeah, I think so. I'm sure you'd be welcome to come back to the apartment with us."

"Yeah, right. I'm sure Natasha would love me third-wheeling on your reunion." Isabella laughed lightly but inside she didn't want to think about their reunion at all. "Jemma's supposed to meet me at the airport. She's got a new apartment arranged for us that she's excited to show me." She looked at Thomas carefully before she continued. "So, I take it Natasha is done being mad at you?"

"Well, that remains to be seen. She *was* pretty upset about me missing the wedding."

Isabella was quiet, not sure of what to say.

"Iz."

"Yeah?"

"I'm not sorry that I went with you. Natasha's going to have to accept the fact that you're always going to be in my life and that, with some things, you're always going to come first. This trip was a big deal to you and I got to meet your father."

Isabella felt tears stinging her eyes. She reached out to touch Thomas's arm. "I know. I still can't believe it. He's great, isn't he? And Annie. Wow, I still can't believe I have a sister."

Thomas was smiling. "It's great, Iz. Really."

"And thanks again—so much—for coming. I'm not sure that I would have been able to do without you."

"You would have. But I'm glad I was there."

"And I do hope that Natasha won't stay mad at you for long."

"She won't." Thomas winked. "I have my ways, ya know."

Isabella's stomach fell. "I'm sure you do."

Minutes later they were off the plane, through

passport control, and receiving hugs from Natasha and Jemma, who were waiting together for them. Isabella pasted on a smile, excited to see Jemma and equally as unexcited to watch Thomas with Natasha.

"She's still mad." Jemma whispered into Isabella's ear. "I feel kinda sorry for Thomas."

Isabella cringed. "I guess he's ready for it." She pulled away from Jemma's hug. "Oh, I can't wait to have a good chat—to hear about everything."

"I can't wait to hear about everything! And to show you our new apartment. You're gonna love it, and it will be fun to be in London right now. It's cold but so festive. It's making me really excited about Christmas."

"I'm excited too. Thanks for meeting me." Isabella gave Jemma one last squeeze and then she gave a quick hug to Natasha and an equally quick hug to Thomas. "I guess we're going separate ways on the tube. Get together later? Tomorrow night maybe."

"Yeah, that sounds great—"

Natasha gave Thomas a look. "Well, actually, honey, we have that party tomorrow night." She turned back toward Isabella. "We'll call you."

Isabella nodded. She didn't think she'd be seeing Thomas for a while—not if Natasha had anything to say about it. "Okay. Sure. We'll talk to you two later."

PAULA KAY

CHAPTER 29

Isabella settled into a big overstuffed chair in their new rented living room, waiting for Jemma to bring her the cup of tea she was preparing for them. The apartment was perfect. It had everything that they'd loved about their place in Paris—great views, plenty of room, and a cozy atmosphere.

Isabella noticed Jemma's easel set up by one of the big windows, and not far from it a nice big table and comfortable office chair. She smiled, thinking about Jemma setting up a work station for her. She was taking a break from writing, but she did have a lot of promotional things to learn about with the launch of her first book.

"How's your painting going?" Isabella gestured toward the easel as Jemma set the tea and plate of small sandwiches down on the table near where Isabella sat. "Ooh, yum. And I must say, you're becoming very British with your tea and sandwiches, aren't you?"

They both laughed.

"I'm trying." Jemma smiled as she settled into the chair opposite Isabella. "And the painting is going well.

I'm almost finished."

"With your presents?" Isabella smiled. She thought it was a wonderful idea that Jemma had had, to give paintings as gifts for Christmas.

"Yep. Only one more to go—for Thomas, actually. I was hoping you could help me with that idea."

"Aww, that's very sweet of you. I'm having my doubts that Thomas will come for Christmas, though. We'll probably have to have a little celebration with him—with them—here before we go."

"Oh. That's too bad. Maybe if he could bring Natasha? I'm sure your grandparents wouldn't mind. They've added on that big guest house to the property, so there's plenty of room now."

Isabella crinkled her nose. She couldn't help it. As much as she'd like Thomas to come for Christmas and meet everyone, she couldn't imagine having Natasha there. She didn't want her there, regardless of how that sounded.

"Bella." Jemma was laughing at her.

"Well, I'm sorry. She's not really that friendly toward me, is she? I want Thomas there—sure, but not if it means bringing her." She looked back at Jemma and shrugged her shoulder. "So I'm a terrible person. I can't help the way I feel. You saw how she was toward me at the airport."

Jemma had a funny look on her face.

"What?"

"Well, her boyfriend did just spend almost an entire week away with another woman. She's probably just jealous. And rightfully so?"

"Is that a question?" Isabella felt her face going warm.

"Of course it's a question. How *was* it being away with Thomas? You know, I'm convinced that there's much more to this so-called friendship between the two of you. Anyone can see it, Bella."

Isabella looked down to stare into the cup she was drinking out of. She didn't know yet how she was feeling about her time away with Thomas. Nothing had happened between them, yet she felt that something might have happened. But was that just her imagination or was it something she should finally share with Jemma?

"San Francisco was great. I have so much to tell you—about everything—my father, sister, and the house! Jemma, can you believe that I saw the house that my mother grew up in? It was—"

"—Are you officially changing the subject on me now then?" Jemma was grinning, but Isabella knew that she'd be talking to her about everything now. "I mean, of course I want to hear all about your dad, but can we just stay on the subject of what happened between you and Thomas? Because by the look on your face, I'm pretty sure that there's something you're not telling me."

Isabella sighed and took a bite of her sandwich. "Well, okay. So, nothing happened—not really. But we had a great time and this especially awesome day shopping in downtown San Francisco. It felt like old times together and I guess, if I'm being honest, something feels different to me."

"Different how?"

Isabella cringed, reluctant to say the words out loud. Having the thoughts in her head were one thing, but speaking them to another person somehow meant that she had to learn to deal with them—to stifle them somehow. "Okay, Jemma. You promise you're not going to hold this against me, as I'm really not sure exactly how I'm feeling, but really I do think I need to talk about this with someone."

"And I'm your someone." Jemma grinned. "Go on. What happened?"

"Okay, so nothing really happened. It's more about how I'm feeling. I can't believe I'm saying this, but there were definitely moments where I wanted something to happen—moments where I didn't want to look at Thomas as only my best friend any more. But, Jemma—it's not more than that. And I don't want to ruin our friendship. That's the last thing I want and I'd never do anything to jeopardize that. You know?"

Jemma was nodding her head. "Yeah, I do get that. But what if Thomas is…"

"What? Is what?"

"What if he's the one for you? I mean, it could be that you two are soulmates, you know."

"What a romantic idea." Isabella rolled her eyes.

"What? You don't believe in love all of a sudden?" Jemma laughed.

"Oh, I don't know. I guess it's just hard for me not to picture Thomas as my friend—when you get right down to it, I mean." She shook her head. "And honestly. I shouldn't even be talking like this. It would appear that Thomas is in love with Natasha."

Jemma was shaking her head. "I don't know. I've seen the way he looks at you."

"Really? You're not just saying that?"

"Really. I'd put money on the fact that he is not interested in you only as a friend—or maybe he's not being honest with himself about it either—but I can see what's there with my own two eyes."

Isabella was quiet, lost in her thoughts about the movie night that she and Thomas had had together in her hotel room. She took a deep breath. "Well, if I'm being honest, I feel like something almost happened one night—actually it was only last night." She laughed, thinking that she needed a good nap soon.

Isabella related the events of the night to Jemma, not leaving anything out, including the fact that she'd wanted something to happen. She'd wanted Thomas to kiss her last night. She told Jemma how he'd been with her the next day and how relieved that she was that nothing had seemed awkward between them.

When she was finished, Jemma was quiet.

"Jem? What are you thinking? I'm crazy, right?"

"No, not all. Now I just feel more sure than ever. But I also get what you're saying about not wanting to ruin the friendship. It's easy for me to tease you about it and want to believe in true love—especially for you." She grinned. "But also the friendship between you two is special—anyone can see that. And well, we know what can happen when relationships don't work out, so I get why there's a lot to think about—a lot to be sure about."

Isabella nodded. "So, I should just leave things alone, right? I mean, I don't know what I'm even talking about. I think it probably is all in my head." She laughed lightly.

"I don't know. I mean the way you're describing how he was with you in your hotel room doesn't sound to me like it was just in your head."

"Well, he has always been pretty affectionate with me. So maybe it really was nothing. It just felt like more to me, I guess. And nothing did happen. So there's that too."

"Well, yeah but who knows what might have happened if you'd not been interrupted by Colin's call, right? It sounds like that was a bit of a mood killer—and something else we need to talk about, by the way."

"Colin? I'm pretty sure that's over. Well, I haven't told him that yet, I guess, but I'm really not interested. And I should just be honest with him about it." She was thoughtful. "But you are right that the phone call did seem to have an effect on the night. That's for sure."

"Time will tell, I guess. Maybe a lot will depend on

how things go between him and Natasha now that he's back. Oh and by the way, I'm pretty sure Natasha *is* jealous of you—or at least the relationship that you and Thomas have."

"Well, I do kind of get that impression. She doesn't hide her feelings for me very well, and it's becoming beyond awkward."

"She asked me if I thought you had feelings for him—at the airport just earlier, while we were waiting for you guys."

"Really? What did you say?"

"I just told her that you were best friends—that she didn't have anything to worry about."

Isabella laughed. "Well, good. And the truth. So that's that then. Now, can I tell you about my new family?" She laughed, reaching for her phone so that she could show Jemma all the photos that she'd taken.

"Absolutely. Tell me everything."

PAULA KAY

CHAPTER 30

Isabella bit her bottom lip as she sent the text off to Thomas. It had been over two weeks since they'd gotten back to London and she hadn't seen him since that day. She had the distinct impression that Thomas was avoiding her, and it was starting to make her feel physically sick to her stomach.

Jemma was sure that it had more to do with Natasha, but all Isabella could think about was that last night in San Francisco. Maybe their time together had created more awkwardness than Thomas had first let on.

She looked down to reread her text, annoyed that he wasn't getting back to her.

Can we meet for lunch today? Please?

She jumped as her phone buzzed with an incoming text finally.

Sorry. I don't think I can today.

Isabella felt her heart lurch. This was getting really ridiculous.

Thomas, what's going on? I miss you. Are you mad at me?
No. Not at all. Hold on. I'm going to call you.

Finally. Isabella felt an almost instant sense of relief when her phone buzzed a few seconds later.

"Thomas, what is going on? Seriously!"

"I know. I'm sorry, Iz. I've been terrible."

"Worse than terrible." Isabella laughed lightly, trying to lighten the mood now that they were actually speaking. "Can you meet me for lunch? Please?"

"Hmm."

"Hmm, what? Is Natasha there or something?"

"No, she's at work."

"Okay, so let's go to the diner you were telling me about. My treat."

Thomas laughed on the other end of the line. "Well then, how can I say no to that?"

"Exactly. Your two favorite things."

"And that would be? Burgers and…?"

"Your best friend, of course. Seriously, Thomas, I've really missed you"

"I miss you too, Iz."

They both went quiet for a few seconds before Thomas spoke again. "So, meet me there in an hour? I'll text you the address when we hang up."

"I'll be there."

Isabella hung up feeling relieved. She'd talked herself into all sorts of things over the past few days—all the possible reasons why she might never see her best friend again. In the end, she knew that would never happen. She'd never let it, and she was pretty sure that Thomas wouldn't either.

She pulled on a sweater and grabbed her heavy coat and gloves. The temperatures had decreased a lot lately and she was actually finding that she quite enjoyed London during the winter.

She scribbled a note for Jemma, who was out doing some shopping.

FINALLY meeting up with T for some lunch. Wish me luck! Pizza and a movie in tonight?

Outside, she glanced down at the address that Thomas had sent her, then crossed the street to the tube station.

Isabella looked at the time on her phone as the tube pulled up to her stop. She was fifteen minutes early, just enough time to get her thoughts together. Since Thomas hadn't brought up Christmas to her at all, she assumed it meant that he'd be staying in London, but she'd try one more time just in case he only needed another invitation.

She smiled as she walked up to the diner. It looked very similar to the one back home—their diner—hers and Thomas's. Her eyes scanned the restaurant, settling in on a booth in the back corner.

He was there. He was early. She grinned because it felt so familiar to her—meeting Thomas for lunch at the diner.

Just as she was making her way to the back, Thomas saw her, his whole face lighting up with his wide grin, and it instantly made her nerves disappear. It was only

Thomas. Everything was fine. Everything was going to be just fine.

He stood up to give her a hug. "Iz. I have missed you. I promise."

"Well, you could have fooled me." She laughed lightly but she was ready to scold him a bit for being so absent lately. "What the heck happened to you?"

"I know." He looked down at the menu that the waitress had already delivered.

"Well? You're not going to give me an explanation?" She made sure her voice was light. She wasn't really mad any more, but she was curious to know where his head was at.

"Okay. Promise you're not going to lecture?"

"Mm-hm. Go ahead."

"It's Natasha."

"Okay."

"Oh, I dunno. I guess she's feeling pretty insecure since the whole San Francisco trip—since I chose you over going to her cousin's wedding with her. Her words, not mine. But I guess there's some truth to it. I mean, between you and me, I didn't really want to go to the wedding." He winked.

"So the truth comes out. Now I know why you wanted to go to San Francisco with me. It wasn't about the moral support at all, but the lesser of two evils." Isabella laughed.

Thomas reached out to touch her arm, and Isabella

felt her face flush almost instantly at the shock of his touch.

"No, that's not it at all. But you're teasing. I wanted to be there for you, and really—San Francisco was great, wasn't it?"

Was she imagining the look in his eyes? She shook her arm free from his touch, trying to be discreet about it as she picked up her menu. She looked over at him, and he was looking at her pretty intently still.

"Yeah, it was really great. I'd missed spending time with you, and then San Francisco was almost like old times and then—then I hardly hear from you for two weeks. I wasn't quite sure what to think."

"I know. Natasha was very upset. By the time we'd arrived back here, I thought that she was over the whole thing, but she was very angry with me about it still. She pretty much made me promise that I'd focus on her and I—that if I really cared about her, I'd care about her feelings about you and me hanging out so much."

"I see."

"Okay. I see that look and I know this isn't making a lot of sense to you."

"Well, is Natasha trying to say that you and I can't be friends any more or what? Because I'm not gonna lie, if you choose her over our friendship, yeah it's really going to hurt me, Thomas. I would never do that to you." Before Isabella could even think about holding back, she felt the tears stinging her eyes. She couldn't imagine her life without Thomas in it. She never truly thought it would come to that, and the thought of it was almost unbearable to her.

"Iz, stop. Don't cry." Thomas came around to the opposite side of the booth to sit next to her, wrapping his arms around her before she even knew what was happening. "That's not going to happen. I promise. I figure that she just needs a little time. That's all. Everything's going to be fine. I'll make sure of it, okay? Iz?" He tilted her chin, forcing her to look him in the eye. "I'm never going to choose anyone over you, not even Natasha."

"Promise, you big jerk." Isabella smiled and wiped the rest of her tears away with the sleeve of her sweatshirt.

"Big jerk, huh?" Thomas laughed and scooted back over to his side of the booth just as the waitress came over to take their order. "We'll have two cheeseburgers, two chocolate shakes, and your double order of fries." He smiled at Isabella and winked as he turned back to the waitress. "And can you put extra chili and extra cheese on those fries please? For my lovely date here." He gestured to Isabella.

She could feel her face getting warm as the waitress walked away with their orders. "Yum!"

"I figured you'd like it. So you were saying? About me being a big jerk?"

"Okay, so you're not that big of a jerk, but I don't like this not talking—or even texting, for that matter—one bit."

There was a funny look on Thomas's face.

"What? I feel like there's something you're not telling me."

"So here's where I ask you to try not to judge, okay? But I gotta talk about it to someone—to see how nuts I am."

"Go on."

"Okay, so I caught Natasha looking through my texts the other day."

"Seriously? Thomas, I can't believe that's okay with—"

"—Wait. Let me finish, please." He gave her a little smile. "So, of course I was really upset about it. I mean, I've never really dated anyone who seemed to have so little trust in me, you know?"

Isabella nodded her head. For as long as she'd known Thomas, he'd had no shortage of girlfriends, but one thing she did know about him was that he'd always been faithful to anyone he was exclusive with. He was a very loyal person, a quality that Isabella greatly appreciated about him.

"So anyway, we talked about it and she really opened up to me—about how insecure she was feeling and that she'd been incredibly jealous thinking about me with you on our trip. I'd never seen her like that before. And the truth is, I felt a little bad about being away—or maybe it was more about the great time that you and I had while we were together. I mean, she had at least a bit of a reason to be jealous, don't you think?"

Thomas was looking across the table at her so intently. What exactly was he asking her? Isabella swallowed and tried to calm her racing heart as she thought about how she should answer him.

"I suppose so. If you're talking about the fact that you chose to come with me instead of going to her cousin's wedding. I guess I'd be feeling insecure also—if that was my boyfriend, I mean."

Thomas held his eye contact with her until she looked down at her hands. Was that what he was talking about or was he referring to something else?—to the night on the sofa and the sparks that she could swear were there even though every day since then she'd done her best to talk herself out of thinking about it.

"Okay, so speaking of your boyfriend?"

"We weren't."

Thomas quirked his eyebrow.

"I called it off with Colin, but we weren't talking about me, we were talking about you—and Natasha, right?"

"Did you? Poor guy. Guess he doesn't really have the luck of the Irish when it comes to beautiful American women, huh?" Thomas winked.

Isabella tried not to dwell on the fact that Thomas had just called her beautiful. "So back to you and Natasha—I guess what you're saying is that you're willing to put up with some stuff from her, or what *are* you saying? Are you so in love with her, Thomas?" There, she'd said it before she could even think about stopping herself. She had to know.

Thomas looked like he was thinking about the question. "The answer is I don't know. I mean, I haven't told her that I love her or anything. I guess she's so different from anyone I've ever dated that it's been interesting for me to be with her. I like that she's different. She's driven and smart and quite lovely to look at."

Why? Why did I have to ask him about Natasha? It was all Isabella could do to keep from putting her hands over her ears while Thomas talked about all the things he liked about her. She tried to smile, wanting desperately to change the subject.

"Okay, I get it. You're not sure enough that she isn't the one—not sure enough to not be with her, I mean."

"Well, I don't know if I'd go so far as to say that I think she's the one or anything. It's too soon to tell."

"Well, I feel like I should just ask you this to get it over with now, but I'm pretty sure I know the answer."

"What's that?"

"I'm guessing that you've decided not to join us— Jemma and me—in Tuscany for Christmas, then?" She held her breath in, waiting for him to answer.

He shook his head. "No. As much as I'd love to be with you for the holidays—to meet your whole family—I really think I need to be here this Christmas."

"And Natasha would kill you for leaving." Isabella laughed lightly.

"Iz, that's not fair to her. It is Christmas, right? And—well, between you and me, in my mind, I'm sorta giving us until the holidays—to see how the next few weeks go. Natasha has been a bit stressed lately, but she's been crazy busy at work and I want to just see how things go when she has a few days off."

The waitress put their food down on the table in front of them, and Isabella's stomach growled in response to the burgers and loaded fries in front of her.

"Iz? You're not mad about Christmas, are you?"

She shook her head. "No, I understand. You gotta do what you gotta do. As long as that doesn't require you throwing me to the curb, I'm good with it." She smiled at him to reassure him.

Was she good with it? With Natasha? Not really. But for now she just wanted to enjoy lunch with her best friend.

CHAPTER 31

Isabella came around the dining room table to adjust the last plate setting, admiring the job that she and Jemma had done in terms of making the apartment look festive. There was a small tree lit up in the living room, a big fire going, and Christmas music playing quietly in the background. The smells coming from the kitchen reminded her of her childhood, although unlike her mother, who'd spend hours preparing their holiday meal, Isabella had picked everything up from the local shop with the only instruction being how long to heat the turkey in the oven. She smiled as she stood back to observe the results of her efforts.

"We need one more, right?" Jemma came out of the kitchen holding a set of cutlery and a plate.

"Oh, didn't I tell you? Natasha can't make it." Isabella tried not to look too pleased as she relayed this information. Of course she'd invited both Thomas and Natasha to their London Christmas dinner. She and Jemma were leaving in two days for Tuscany and it was the last chance she'd have to see Thomas for a while.

"Really?" Jemma looked surprised. "No, you didn't tell me this little tidbit of information."

"Yeah, Thomas texted earlier that she'd come down with a headache."

"And she's okay with him coming on his own? Or do you think it was all about getting him to stay home with her?"

"Oh, I don't know. But he's still coming and that's what counts." Isabella grinned. "He did tell me that he wouldn't be able to stay late, but whatever."

She was relieved actually when Thomas had said he was still coming. At first she'd wondered the same—if he was going to cancel on her to stay home with Natasha. She wasn't sure of what her plans would be after the holidays, and not seeing him before they left would have really bothered her, especially because she couldn't wait to give Thomas his gift. She smiled as she placed the wrapped book under the Christmas tree. He had no idea that her book had already been published—she'd been keeping it a secret for weeks now and she couldn't wait to share it with him.

The doorbell rang and she checked her reflection in the hallway mirror before answering. She and Jemma had gone shopping together the day before, wanting to pick up the perfect dresses for their holiday in Tuscany.

Isabella had loved her dress so much, she'd decided to wear it this evening—for Thomas—but she'd not even admitted that to Jemma when they were getting ready earlier. She loved how the red fabric hugged her curves, the low neckline revealing just a bit of cleavage— something that was definitely rare for her. She'd even spent time putting on some make-up and going over her hair with the flatiron, also both rare occurrences. As she looked in the mirror now, she was glad that she'd taken the time.

The doorbell rang a second time.

"Bella, are you getting that or do you want me to?" Jemma called out from the kitchen.

"Nope. I got it right now." She crossed the room to open the door, taking in the sight of Thomas looking very handsome in a suit jacket and slacks. "Hi. Merry Christmas!"

Thomas stood there, holding flowers and gifts in his hands. He stared at her with a grin on his face and Isabella smiled at his reaction, waiting for him to speak.

"Wow! Let me put this down so I can hug you, you gorgeous creature." He laughed as Jemma swooped in to give him a quick kiss on the cheek and take the packages out of his hands.

"Thomas, the flowers are beautiful. I'll just get them in water so we can enjoy them during dinner," Jemma called over her shoulder from the entrance to the kitchen.

Isabella felt awkward all of a sudden as Thomas continued to stare at her, finally pulling her in for a big hug. "Iz, you look really beautiful. I mean—wow!"

Isabella laughed. "I'm not sure if I should be flattered or offended. I must look hideous every other time you see me."

"No, not hideous—never hideous." Thomas laughed, and Isabella didn't miss his eyes taking in her whole body before landing on her face again. "I just—I don't know. I guess I'm a little speechless. You're really beautiful, Iz."

"Thanks. You're sweet to say that, and you look pretty handsome yourself." Isabella turned away before Thomas could see the bright blush that she knew would be apparent on her face. "Come on in. Can I get you a hot cider?" She knew that this was something his family had every holiday season and she was happy to have incorporated it into their evening.

"Really? You know I'd love some." He grinned, poking his head in the kitchen. "And when the heck did you two learn to cook? It smells amazing!"

Jemma eyed Isabella, probably waiting to see if she was going to fess up or make out like they'd become fabulous cooks overnight.

"Okay. We won't lie. It's from the shop. And it does smell pretty fantastic." Isabella laughed, taking Thomas's hand to pull in him toward the living room. "Come sit. Enjoy our lovely tree and dinner will be served momentarily," she said in a very fake British accent.

Thomas obliged as Isabella hurried away and then came back with two warm drinks, to sit across from him.

"How's Natasha doing? I'm sorry she couldn't make

it." She tried to make her face match her words as she noticed that Thomas was not taking his eyes off her.

Was he turning red now? She knew it was entirely possible that Natasha wasn't ill at all, yet it did surprise her that she'd be okay with Thomas coming for dinner on his own. It wasn't like they were alone, though.

"She'll be fine. You know, she's just exhausted, I think from so much work. It's slowing down now in a few days, though."

"Well, I'm glad it didn't change your plan."

"Iz, of course not. We've celebrated every Christmas together since we were teenagers. You can't think I'd miss it—well, as long as we're in the same city, I mean." He smiled at her and his words instantly caused her to flash to so many Christmases as children. Typically, they'd spent the actual holiday with their families separately but then the next day would be just for them. They'd go out for a meal, exchange gifts, and then ice skate or go to the movies or just hang out all day at one of their houses.

"What are you smiling at?"

Thomas's question interrupted her thoughts.

"I was just remembering our youth." Isabella laughed. "Christmases together."

"Good memories, huh, Iz?"

He was still looking at her very intently and she was trying to match his gaze, but she kept having to look away—afraid that he'd see something written on her face that she wasn't sure she wanted him to see.

"Dinner is served, kids."

Saved by Jemma. Isabella stood up to make her way to the dining room, where Jemma already had all the food arranged.

"Jemma. I'm so sorry. I should be helping." Isabella walked toward the kitchen, Jemma stopping her by putting her hand on Isabella's arm.

"Don't be silly. Your job is to entertain our guest." She gestured toward Thomas. "Who's looking mighty fine, I must say." She laughed. "Besides, everything's all ready. Let's sit down."

"It looks wonderful—as do you." Thomas leaned over to give Jemma a hug before sitting down across the table from Isabella.

"Okay, okay. Enough with the compliments. Let's dig in before the food gets cold," Jemma said, handing Thomas the knife to carve the turkey. "Would you do the honors, please?"

Thomas took the knife and carved a good portion of the turkey, and the three piled their plates high with a Christmas dinner that even their mothers would be proud of.

CHAPTER 32

Isabella pushed her chair back from the table. "Wow. I don't know about you guys, but I'm stuffed."

"Me too," Jemma said, getting up from the table to collect the plates.

Isabella and Thomas both stood to help her.

"You two go on. Go make yourself comfortable. I can handle this," Jemma said.

"No. I can help. Or a better idea—let's just get the food put away and you and I can do the rest of the cleanup in the morning. We have presents to do." Isabella smiled, catching Jemma's eye.

"Now that is an idea I can get behind."

Isabella laughed because she knew how much Jemma loved presents—especially the ones she'd been creating over the past few months.

Thomas put his arm around Isabella as they made their way from the kitchen to the living room. He acted as if it was the most natural thing in the world to do, which totally caught Isabella by surprise. She felt her eyes go wide as she noticed Jemma's expression.

"Okay, I'm going to get this little party started by giving you your present," Jemma directed to Thomas as she scooted around the corner to grab the gift that she'd hidden away.

Isabella grinned at Thomas. She loved all of the paintings that Jemma had done, and this had been the last of the ones she'd finished while in London.

Jemma set the large gift on the table in front of Thomas. "I hope you like it. I realize it's big for traveling but I figure you can ship it home to your parent's house—if you end up leaving Natasha—leaving London, I mean." Jemma turned bright red as soon as the words had left her mouth.

Thomas and Isabella looked at one another and burst out laughing.

"Yes, for sure. I can send it to my parents, no worries."

"Or he'll hang it in Natasha's apartment." Isabella winked at Jemma.

Thomas ripped the paper off and held the painting of the London city skyline up in front of him. "It's great. Isabella told me you were a great artist, but this is really spectacular." He set the painting back down on the table and walked around it to give Jemma a big hug. "Thanks so much. It's perfect."

Thomas turned and bent down to retrieve his gifts that Jemma had placed under the tree. He handed the larger one to Jemma and the smaller one to Isabella.

"Oh, very nice." Jemma exclaimed over the high-quality artist's pad and specialty colored pencils. She stood up and walked to where Thomas was standing by the tree to give him a quick kiss on the cheek. "I love it and it's perfect for traveling." She gestured toward Isabella's gift, still unopened in her lap. "Go on, Bella. Open yours."

Isabella grinned as she tore the paper away from her gift, her fingers going across the fine leather that was the cover of the beautiful new journal that Thomas had gotten for her.

"I'm sure you already have one that you're writing in, but maybe it can start off the new year for you. I read recently how important journaling is for writers, so it's meant to be something that will support your wildly successful career as an author."

"It's perfect, and thank you for supporting my somewhat wacky career changes." Isabella laughed and walked over to give Thomas a big hug. "Speaking of wacky career changes…" She grinned over at Jemma, still sitting on the sofa watching them, as she bent down to pick up her gift for Thomas.

He took the present from her, smiling as he felt around the edges. "Hmm, is it that new thriller novel I said I've been wanting to read—that new fantasy novel that you wanted me to read or—"

"Just open it!" Isabella laughed as she stood beside

him waiting and watching his face as he started to peel back the paper.

"*Her Mother's Eyes...*" His eyes scanned the whole cover and then turned toward Isabella.

She knew she was grinning like a madwoman, and she loved the expression on his face.

"Iz. Your book! Why didn't you tell me? Wow, it's so great. I'm so unbelievably proud of you."

The look on Thomas's face meant everything to her—it was the look he'd given her when he first saw her at the door earlier times ten. It was a look that made her heart beat fast, and before she even knew what was happening he'd grabbed her in a big hug, pulling away for a second to look into her eyes before she felt his lips squarely on her own, tentative at first and then with an unexpected burst of intensity.

The kiss must have only lasted a few seconds, but it felt like longer. It felt like everything she'd ever wanted, everything she'd ever needed from another person.

As their lips found their way apart, she could feel his heartbeat against her, the scent of him making her feel dizzy for wanting another taste of his lips on hers.

A sound from the coffee table brought Isabella out of the daydream she seemed to be caught up in. She opened her eyes, thrilled that she was, in fact, in Thomas's arms. She took a slight step back, putting her hands gently on his chest as she looked up into his eyes.

He reached over to push her hair back away from her

cheek, his eyes not leaving hers.

She was afraid to breathe for fear of breaking the spell that they both seemed to be under.

"Wow." Thomas smiled, pulling her back to his chest.

She nestled her face against the sweater he wore. She fit so perfectly in his arms. Did he feel it too? How had they never realized this before?

Finally, Thomas seemed to notice that Jemma had moved from the living room to the kitchen. He squeezed Isabella to him one more time and took a step back. "Wow. I'm not sure where that came from," he whispered. "I hope we didn't just make Jemma feel too incredibly awkward."

"She'll be okay." Isabella could barely get the words out as she willed herself to act normal.

"Thank you for my present," he finally said, holding the book in his hand as he started to walk toward the door. "I should probably be getting home."

Isabella followed him to the door, completely unsure of what to say or do in the moment. She couldn't let him leave like that, not without saying something about what had just happened between him.

He opened the door.

Say something, Isabella.

"Thomas?"

He turned to face her, his hand still on the doorknob.

"Are you okay? Are we going to be okay after—after that?" Her voice was shaking. They had to be more than okay after a kiss like that. She knew in that instant that things wouldn't be able to go back to normal—not for her, anyway.

He looked at her for a moment and then pulled her to him with his free hand, kissing the top of her head. "Merry Christmas, Iz. We'll talk tomorrow, okay?"

Isabella nodded, her mind racing as she locked the door behind him after he'd gone. Before she'd even had a chance to turn around, Jemma was by her side, her eyes wide.

"Bella, what the heck was that all about?" She was smiling as she pulled Isabella by the hand over to the sofa to sit down.

"You saw?"

"Uh—hello! One minute I was watching you two unwrap presents, and the next you were lip-locked in the hottest kiss I've seen in a while."

"I think I'm going to throw up." Isabella was not exaggerating. She felt sick to her stomach wondering what was going to happen next between her and Thomas. She had the suspicion that it wasn't going to go well for her at all.

"No. No, Bella. Don't say that. You don't mean that it was bad, do you? I mean, in my mind that kiss just reaffirmed everything I've ever said to you about how much I think you and Thomas need to be together. You were like a magnet in his arms." Jemma laughed.

"But what now, Jem? Now I'm going to be left

freaking out about our entire relationship again, and right before we're leaving and—"

"—Wait! Stop! What did you think about the kiss? About being in his arms like that?"

Isabella looked at her friend, her hands literally shaking, and relived every instant of the kiss in her mind like a movie in slow motion. "Wow. It was really amazing." She smiled. Dare she just enjoy the way Thomas had made her feel only minutes earlier? "It felt oddly right, like it was meant to happen, you know?"

"Duh. That's because he's your soulmate." Jemma laughed, but then stopped herself, probably because of the look on Isabella's face. "Don't get freaked out. There's no reason to."

"Not yet, you mean." Isabella sighed.

"Well, how did you leave it? What did he say when he was leaving?"

"He kissed me on top of my head and wished me a Merry Christmas."

"Okay…"

"And well, he did say that we'd talk tomorrow."

"Well, that's good. I'm sure he'll call you and you'll work everything out. Will you?"

"You're asking me?" Isabella felt annoyed by the question. "Jemma, just a few days ago he was telling me that he really wanted to try to work things out with Natasha—that he did have strong feelings for her, at least strong enough to give their relationship a good chance.

So, I really don't know what there'd be to work out." She shook her head. "Oh, I can't talk about it any more. Do you mind if I go to bed? Sorry, Jem. I just need some time to myself to think about everything."

Jemma leaned forward to give Isabella a big hug. "Not at all. And please try not to worry. I say enjoy it." She laughed as she got up to walk to the kitchen. "And sweet dreams, Bella." She turned around to wink at Isabella, who offered her a weak smile in return.

Isabella got up to make her way to the bedroom, finally allowing herself a smile again as she lay on top of her bed, closed her eyes, and let herself remember every second of Thomas's kiss.

CHAPTER 33

Isabella carefully refolded her pile of sweaters for about the tenth time, trying to put Thomas and the fact that he'd not contacted her yet out of her mind. It was nearly three o'clock in the afternoon, and she and Jemma were flying to Florence in the morning.

They were leaving the apartment and London, neither of them sure where they'd head after Italy. Isabella still wanted to see more of Europe—there were still places on Arianna's map that they'd not been to yet—before she headed to Southeast Asia. That was the tentative plan in her head anyway. But lately Jemma had been talking a lot about visiting Gigi and Douglas in Guatemala, so that was a possibility as well.

Or they'd go their separate ways for a while, something Isabella felt a little unsure about. She'd grown so close to Jemma and they traveled so well together, but she also realized that traveling alone might help her to grow in ways that she hadn't yet.

Originally, she'd thought that Thomas might be

joining them, but his trip seemed to have stalled out in London—at least for the time being. Isabella sighed as she picked up her phone to check her messages again.

"No word yet?" Jemma stood in Isabella's doorway.

Isabella shook her head. "Nope."

"Maybe you should text him. Does he know we're leaving in the morning?"

"He knows." Isabella put down the sweater she was folding. "Jem, I feel sick about it all. And honestly, I'm starting to get pretty angry with him—the more time that goes by today. And I don't want to leave London being angry with Thomas. What a mess."

Jemma looked thoughtful. "The timing does stink and I'd be shocked if you don't hear from him, but—"

Isabella jumped as her phone buzzed with a text on her dresser. She crossed the room to pick it up, reading the note from Thomas.

Can you meet me at the diner in 30 minutes? Sorry for the late notice.

Before she could think too much about it, she sent off her reply.

Sure. See you in 30.

"Thomas, I take it?"

"Yep, he wants me to meet him in thirty minutes, so I gotta run. I doubt I'll be long."

Isabella walked to the hall closet to get her coat and hat, pulling them on quickly with Jemma following behind her. She turned toward her before stepping out into the hallway. "At this point, I just want to get this over with—make sure everything is okay between us. Wish me luck?"

Jemma leaned in to give her a quick hug. "Everything's going to be fine. Just be honest with him—about your feelings, I mean. And good luck."

Isabella stepped outside, enjoying the cool air as it hit her face. She had a few minutes, so she decided to walk a few blocks to another tube stop, trusting that it would help her to clear her head a little bit.

What was she feeling about Thomas? About the kiss?

She'd tossed and turned all night long, replaying it in her mind over and over again. She wouldn't lie to herself about it, but she didn't want to get solely caught up in the emotions of it either. Nothing had changed in terms of her not wanting to risk her friendship with Thomas, but had they already crossed a line that they couldn't step back from?

She shook her head as if it would help her to make sense of all the thoughts scattered in her mind. She couldn't think about it any more. Not until she was face-to-face with him.

When Isabella saw Thomas sitting in the diner twenty minutes later, she felt both relieved and anxious. He smiled at her as he stood, his grin as wide as ever, but there was something different about the way he hugged her. He was tense. She could feel it in his body.

"Hey, you. How's the packing going? Are you all ready for tomorrow?"

She nodded. "Making progress, but I still have a bit more to do."

Their eyes met across the table.

"Well, I won't keep you too long. I've got somewhere to be tonight as well."

The words cut her. She wanted Thomas to be with her—she wanted him to take her in his arms and offer to come sit with her while she packed. She wanted him to come to Italy with her or to make her promise that she'd come back here to him. She wanted all of that, but in response to his comment, she only nodded. More important than that whole fantasy was the fact that she didn't want to lose her best friend.

They ordered sodas and fries, in agreement that neither of them was hungry for more than that.

Isabella played with the wrapper from her straw, willing Thomas to talk. She'd lost all ability to be able to have any kind of normal conversation with him as she watched him across the table from her.

"So, Iz—about last night."

"Mm-hm."

"I really don't know what came over me. When you showed me your book, I was just—I dunno—overcome with emotion, I guess. I'm so proud of you and how far you've come. And the dress you were wearing—the way you looked last night. I'm still trying to make sense of it all, if I'm being honest."

"Thomas, what does that mean exactly? I don't know if you just go around kissing friends that you feel proud of like that." She laughed lightly, not wanting to make the conversation any more uncomfortable than it already was.

Thomas seemed to be struggling a bit to answer her, and for a minute Isabella just wanted to shake it all off, making everything normal again between them. But could things ever be normal again? She sighed and Thomas looked over at her intently.

"What, Iz? What are you thinking? Are you mad at me? For being so impulsive?"

She thought about it for a second before answering him—his choice of words. It had been impulsive. She believed that he'd had no intention of kissing her last night before it had actually happened.

She studied him for a moment. He looked so unsure of himself, so uncomfortable. She hated this. She wouldn't leave things like this. Their friendship meant too much to her. If he wanted to just sweep everything under the rug, then she'd do so now. Hopefully things could go back to normal, but all they could do was try at this point.

"Look, Thomas. I'm not mad at you. If anything, I'm mad at myself. It shouldn't have happened, period. It did—for whatever reason—and hopefully we can just forget about it and move on. It seems like neither of us wants to jeopardize our friendship and I know you're trying to figure things out with Natasha, so that's that."

She smiled at him—mostly fake, but also willing herself to accept everything she'd just said out loud herself.

She certainly felt resolute with the things she was saying. She had other things to do, family to get ready to see. She'd spent too much time working on herself and figuring out what she wanted in her life to let this be a huge stumbling block for her.

"Thomas? Why don't you look happy?" She laughed and flicked his arm across the table. "Everything is fine. I'm going to Tuscany tomorrow, it's the holidays, it's a time to be merry, right?" She flashed him her biggest grin and somewhere inside of her she started to believe that everything really was going to be just fine, that they'd recover from the mistake they'd made the night before.

Thomas was looking at her, a smile finally making its way back to his face. "You're really something, you know, Iz. I do know one thing for sure."

"What's that?"

"You're the best friend I've ever had. I don't want to lose that. Not ever."

"Well, good. Don't do anything to make me hate you and that probably will never happen." Isabella took a big last drink from her soda and grabbed a couple of the last fries. "Now, let's get our bill. I gotta get the show on the road with my packing."

They left the diner, Thomas paying the bill while Isabella waited for him outside.

"I'll walk you to the tube."

"Its just across the street." She winked at him. "Go home. Everything's cool. I promise."

"Are you sure?"

"Yeah, of course I'm sure." And she was sure. She'd already pushed everything aside, compartmentalizing it all in her brain so that she could move on and get done what she had to get done the rest of the day. "Have a great Christmas, Thomas. Give Natasha my best."

Thomas reached over to give her a big hug and she felt his hands on her hair as he squeezed her to him. "I really do adore you, you know."

She pulled her head back so that she could look him in the eye. "Oh, I know you do." She laughed at the expression on his face. "And I adore you too, you big goofball."

"Merry Christmas, Iz. Have a great time with your family. Let's plan to video chat, okay?"

"Of course. See you later." She smiled at him one last time and then crossed the street to the tube.

As she stood at the top of the steps, she looked over to see Thomas still standing on the sidewalk looking at her. She waved, wondering if it would be the last time in a long while that she'd see him.

PAULA KAY

CHAPTER 34

Isabella leaned her seat back, turning her head to look out the window. She really was getting to be a pro with the whole flying thing. She smiled, remembering how scared she'd been the first time that she'd gotten on the plane with Douglas so long ago. She still couldn't believe that he'd gone all the way to Connecticut to get her, to bring her to be with them all in Tuscany. She didn't understand until she met him why her mother's lawyer would go through all that trouble—but he hadn't been just Arianna's lawyer at all, he'd been part of the family—part of her family now.

She jumped slightly when she felt Jemma's hand on her arm.

"Bella, are you okay?"

She turned her head to look at Jemma sitting beside her. "Yeah, I'm fine. Why?"

"Well, because you've not said a word to me about how things went with Thomas at the diner yesterday. I don't want to pry, but you know I'm dying to find out."

Isabella had told Jemma that she didn't want to talk about it—about Thomas—when she'd gotten back from the diner the night before. She'd had too much to do and too many other things to think about. They'd spent the rest of the night packing and enjoying a final late dinner at one of their favorite neighborhood restaurants, talking about seeing everyone in Italy and ideas that they had about their future travel plans.

It had been the perfect way to end their final night in London, a perfect way for Isabella to move forward with good memories and the promise of leaving any mistakes behind her when she left.

"Sorry about last night, Jem. And thanks for giving me some space about the whole thing."

"Of course."

"Everything is fine between Thomas and me."

"Okay. Fine as in we're still best friends or fine as in he's breaking up with Natasha to finally be with who he's *supposed* to be with?" Jemma laughed.

"Jem, don't. Please." Isabella really needed for Jemma to get what she was saying in order to move on from everything. "It's really okay. I don't know if Thomas is going to end up with Natasha—in the long run, I mean. I don't think he has a clue about that either. But both of us believe that our friendship is the most important thing— that the accidental kiss was basically a huge mistake and one that we need to forget about."

"Bella!" The look on Jemma's face was one of shock. "What?"

"The *accidental* kiss. Come on. I was there. That kiss

was no accident. You're both kidding yourself if you're saying that there wasn't something to that kiss."

Isabella breathed in deeply. It was going to be difficult to get over it, unless she had the full support of Jemma. She certainly didn't need Jemma reminding her about her own doubts and she really did have to move on—for the sake of her own sanity. She turned in her seat so that she could face Jemma—look her in the eyes.

"Please listen to me, okay?"

Jemma nodded and Isabella guessed that she was fighting the urge to say a lot more.

"I really need to get over this idea that there's anything other than friendship between me and Thomas. If you want me to have any hope of ever falling in love myself, you'll help me in this and not make it harder for me, okay? Jem?"

"Okay. Of course I don't want to not be supportive. You know I want you to be happy and of course that includes love. I'm all for that. I just don't want you to make a mistake, you know?"

"I know, but that's what I'm saying. Thomas and I both think that what happened the other night was a mistake. Now we just gotta make things right again."

"Okay. If you say so."

"It's alright if you don't agree with me, but please can we stop talking about it? I really do want to move on." Isabella hesitated for a moment before reaching for her mother's leather journal that she'd stuck in her seat pocket. She opened it to one of the letters that Arianna had written to her—the one about the things that her mother had wanted for her. "Here. Read this." Isabella handed the journal to Jemma, and then watched her face as she read it.

Jemma glanced at Isabella and then read a section of the letter out loud. "'I want you to always have hope within your heart—to know that no matter what the past holds or who you were yesterday, your future can be whatever you imagine it to be. What are your hopes and dreams, Bella? Do you know?'" Jemma stopped reading to look over at her. "Wow. I can almost hear Ari asking those questions."

Isabella nodded. "I know. Me too, even though I've never heard her speak. I feel like her letters are guiding me in a way. I'm not sure if that sounds weird."

"Like the map." Jemma was grinning at her. "I think Ari would love that. It's kinda like she left a treasure map for you of sorts—all these new places you're going and being able to read these letters of advice from her. I think it's pretty cool that she did that for you."

"I do too, and you know what?"

"What?"

"It does help me. Rereading her words to me again is helping to put everything into perspective—about what's important as it pertains to me and my family, but also in regards to my relationship with Thomas."

Jemma looked thoughtful. "And do you know? What

your hopes are? That's a loaded question, huh?"

Isabella nodded. "I'm not sure that I'm supposed to know that now—at our age, I mean. But I feel like I'm getting a better idea of it. I think my writing is part of that. And I do feel really hopeful. The stuff with Thomas isn't going to change that. I won't let it. And eventually I'll find love like what my mother described in the letter too. But I'm okay waiting for that, you know?"

Jemma nodded. "Yes, I do know. I'm okay waiting for that myself—for the right one."

Isabella was well aware of Jemma's past boyfriend and everything bad that had happened between them—and also all the ways that Jemma had changed since that relationship.

"Well, you deserve someone amazing. That's for sure. And there's a lot happening right now—a lot of good thing, right?" Isabella grinned. "We're gonna see everyone in just a few hours, and I can't wait until Christmas. I feel like Christmas in Tuscany is going to be magical, you know? I've not had that yet—with everyone, I mean. And I just want to enjoy it—to celebrate with everyone that I love."

Jemma grinned back at her. "Alright then. I won't say another word about what happened between you and Thomas. I hear you loud and clear. If you do want to talk about it—about anything—you know I'm always here for you."

"I know. And thank you for that."

"And yes. We all have a lot to celebrate this Christmas—the most important thing being the fact that it's our first Christmas with you. Everyone is beyond excited about it. I talked to Lia and Gigi yesterday and—well, let's just say that Gigi warmed me that Lia may have gone a little overboard with the preparations."

Isabella laughed. "I really can't wait."

"And your book, Bella. Everyone is going to be so excited and so incredibly proud of you."

"My book and your paintings. We've been quite busy since we saw them last, huh?"

Jemma nodded. "And on that note, I'm gonna take a little nap. With all the packing and trip preparations, suddenly I'm feeling exhausted."

"Me too." Isabella reclined her seat and as she put her head back against it, she thought again about Arianna's letters to her and how far she'd come since she'd first read her mother's journal.

She smiled, releasing the final remnants of worry about Thomas, her book, her future—everything that she'd been hanging on to for the past few weeks. In its place she allowed herself to be filled with all the hope that her mother had ever wanted for her.

Yes, there was certainly a lot to be hopeful for, starting with this Christmas reunion in Tuscany.

ABOUT THE AUTHOR

Paula Kay spent her childhood in a small town alongside the Mississippi River in Wisconsin. (Go Packers!) As a child, she used to climb the bluffs and stare out across the mighty river—dreaming of far away lands and adventures.

Today, by some great miracle (and a lot of determination) she is able to travel, write and live in multiple locations, always grateful for the opportunity to meet new people and experience new cultures.

She enjoys Christian music, long chats with friends, reading (and writing) books that make her cry and just a tad too much reality TV.

Paula loves to hear from her readers and can be contacted via her website where you can also download a complimentary book of short stories.

PaulaKayBooks.com

ALL TITLES BY PAULA KAY

http://Amazon.com/author/paulakay

The Complete Legacy Series

Buying Time
In Her Own Time
Matter of Time
Taking Time
Just in Time
All in Good Time

A Map for Bella:

Bella's Hope
Bella's Heart
Bella's Home

Christmas Reunion (A Legacy Series Novella)
*Chronologically, "Christmas Reunion" come after
"Bella's Hope" above

Visit the author website at PaulaKayBooks.com to get
on the notification list for new releases, information
about new series and to also receive the complimentary
download of "The Bridge: A Collection of Short Stories."

17720454R00139

Printed in Poland
by Amazon Fulfillment
Poland Sp. z o.o., Wrocław